T0126906

The Midnight Moon

by

Gerri Hill

Bella
BOOKS

2014

Bella Books, Inc.
P.O. Box 10543
Tallahassee, FL 32302

First Bella Books Edition 2014

Editor: Medora MacDougall
Cover Designer: Judith Fellows

ISBN: 978-1-59493-410-0

Other Bella Books by Gerri Hill

Artist's Dream
At Seventeen
Behind the Pine Curtain
The Cottage
Coyote Sky
Dawn of Change
Devil's Rock
Gulf Breeze
Hell's Highway
Hunter's Way
In the Name of the Father
Keepers of the Cave
The Killing Room
Love Waits
No Strings
One Summer Night
Partners
The Rainbow Cedar
The Scorpion
Sierra City
Snow Falls
Storms
The Target
Weeping Walls

About the Author

Gerri Hill has twenty-five published works, including the 2013 GCLS winner *Snow Falls*, 2011 and 2012 GCLS winners *Devil's Rock* and *Hell's Highway*, and the 2009 GCLS winner *Partners*, the last book in the popular Hunter Series, as well as the 2012 Lambda finalist *Storms*. Hill's love of nature and of being outdoors usually makes its way into her stories as her characters often find themselves in beautiful natural settings. When she isn't writing, Gerri and her longtime partner, Diane, keep busy at their log cabin in East Texas tending to their two vegetable gardens, orchard and five acres of piney woods. They share their lives with two Australian Shepherds and an assortment of furry felines.

CHAPTER ONE

Peyton Watts gave her assistant a puzzled look. "A vacation? Alone? To a lesbian hot spot?" She shook her head. "Don't be ridiculous."

"How long are you going to continue to sulk over her?"

"Sulk? I'm certainly not sulking. It's been eight months since...since—" She threw up her hands. "It was my best friend, for God's sake. Have I said that?"

"About a hundred times," Susan murmured.

"She was sleeping with my best friend," Peyton continued. "Right under my nose. Did I tell you that?"

Susan gave her an amused smile. "A hundred times. And as I said before, she wasn't really your best friend."

Peyton lowered her head to her desk and closed her eyes, still able to see them in her bed; Alicia with a stunned expression on her face and Vicky trying to lay the blame on her, as if *she* had been the one in bed with her best friend. "Oh, God, I am still sulking, aren't I?" She opened her eyes to peek at Susan. "I kinda miss her."

"Oh, Peyton, don't. She was a conniving bitch. I never did like her. I told you that from the very beginning."

Peyton lifted her head and smiled. "No. I was talking about Alicia, not Vicky."

"Well, I did like Alicia, I guess, but I wasn't around her all that much. And you've got to stop thinking of her as your best friend."

"I know." Peyton sat back in her chair and let out a heavy sigh. "God, I hate women."

"Well, you could always join my team," Susan said with a laugh. "I could have Michael set you up."

"I don't hate them *that* much." She turned to her and smiled. "So you think I need a vacation, huh?"

Susan nodded. "Yes. Tax season is over finally. I know you're exhausted."

Peyton nodded. Yes, she was exhausted. January through April was always hectic in an accounting firm. But this year she'd had no reason to go home each evening and she'd put in nearly obscene hours. She told herself it was her firm and she needed to lead by example, but even she knew she'd taken it to the extreme. It was the house. She should have sold it after Vicky moved out, but it was in the hills of West Austin and close to her office. Even though they'd lived together only five years—five years, three months and a handful of days—Vicky had put her stamp on it. Vicky had the green thumb and kept the flower beds filled with seasonal plants. Vicky was a chef and the kitchen was stocked with every cooking gadget imaginable. Vicky supplied them with delicious meals and frequent dinner parties. That part, she did miss.

Now she hired a landscaping crew to plant her flowers and maintain the lawn. And meals? Oh, she cooked some. But cooking for one was depressing. She usually grabbed something on her way home or, less frequently, had dinner out with friends. Those were the times she missed Alicia the most. They'd known each other several years before Vicky had come into her life. Still, they'd made time for dinner at least once a week. And even though, deep down, she knew it was Vicky's fault, she couldn't bring herself to forgive Alicia. They hadn't spoken since the night she'd caught them in bed, although Alicia had reached out to her—at least in the beginning. Now, eight months had passed and she doubted they could ever get their friendship back. Vicky had moved on too, already living with someone else, an attorney who Peyton had once dated herself.

She shook her head slowly, hating her life at that moment. She'd be thirty-five years old by the end of summer and her personal life was as unsettled as it'd been in her twenties. She looked at Susan and gave her a weak smile. Susan had been working for her ever since Peyton bought the firm from Mr. Neely, eight years now. She knew that Susan was an excellent judge of character and she should have trusted her when it came to Vicky. Susan had told her once she thought Vicky was devious. That, of course, turned out to be true. And now that Vicky was living with someone else, it was brought to her attention that Vicky's past lovers were all professional women, all with nice homes and equally nice incomes. And Peyton had succumbed to her charm as easily as the others apparently.

"So tell me about this beach vacation," she prompted.

Susan reached for Peyton's laptop. "It's on Mustang Island. Port Aransas," she said as she pulled up a browser.

"How do you know about it? You're not gay," Peyton said.

"I heard about it from Jeannie."

"Who's Jeannie?"

"My cousin. She and a group of her friends went down there in March." She spun the laptop toward her, showing her a picture of a brightly colored umbrella stabbed in the sand with two women lying under it. "Right on the beach. It was an old three-story hotel that was closed. They renovated it, then added these cute cabanas and put in two pools," she said, bringing up another picture. "One is clothing optional. I'm sure that's the one you'll hang out at," she said with a laugh.

"Right," Peyton said dryly. The photos did look inviting, though, as beautiful, tan women lounged around the pools. "And it's marketed to lesbians?"

"Yes. Jeannie said they had a great time there. I think you should try it."

Peyton hesitated. "I'm not sure going there alone sounds all that exciting," she said. "There's probably going to be no one there other than couples." She pointed to the advertisement. "Romantic getaway. My getaway would be anything *but* romantic," she said.

"I wasn't suggesting this to you because it would be romantic. I was thinking it'd be a great place for you to go and recharge and get away from Austin for a week."

But still she hesitated. While it looked fun and all of the women in the pictures were smiling and happy, it wasn't really her kind of scene. She'd never been a beach lover and she had her own pool at her house. It would seem to be a waste to go down to Port Aransas just to sit by a pool. Of course, the cabanas looked inviting and the palm trees made it all appear as if it was a tropical paradise. She supposed sitting in the sun relaxing with a fruity drink would be refreshing.

"Well?"

Peyton stared at the scene, trying to picture herself there. "What the hell. I guess I do need to get away."

CHAPTER TWO

Logan Weaver knocked twice on the office door before opening it and peeking her head inside. Emma was on the phone and waved her in with a nod and a smile. Logan went to the window that overlooked the pool, her gaze traveling over the handful of women who were either splashing in the water or lounging in the sun. Sitting nearest the window on a chaise lounge pulled away from the others was a pretty blonde, her eyes covered by sunglasses but her deep red bikini offering a glimpse of a tantalizing body.

"She came in this morning," Emma said as she joined her at the window. "She was very reserved. Not your type at all."

"You told me I couldn't hit on your guests," Logan reminded her.

"I did, didn't I." Emma came closer and pulled her into a hug. "You're early, sis. Where's Jay and Drew?"

"They had a project come up," she said. "They can't make it."

"That's too bad. I was looking forward to seeing them again." She tossed her a set of keys. "But I guess that frees up the suite then. I had someone ask about it yesterday."

Logan looked at the key, noting the number. It was the single room she normally stayed in when she came alone. "That's fine. I may not stay the whole week anyway. Ted's been complaining about his lack of fishing days and threatening retirement again."

Emma smiled. "And how is your father?"

"He's good," she said. "You talk to Mom lately?"

"Last week. She and Dad were heading to Florida for their annual trip." Emma eyed her. "You really should call her more often."

"I know. Time gets away, though. You were always the better daughter," she said.

"Stepdaughter," Emma corrected.

Logan smiled affectionately at her, this woman who'd been in her life for as long as she could remember. Logan was five when her mother remarried and they moved in with Emma and Dave. Emma's own mother had died in an automobile accident a few years earlier. Emma was only a year older and they'd fallen into a fast friendship, one that had endured through the years, even in high school when they both discovered they were gay...and both wanted to hang out with Missy Graham, the cute tennis player.

Their adult lives took them different places, though. While her mother and Dave were happily married, Logan's father, Ted, was quite the opposite. Taking over his father's painting business in Austin, he'd nearly run it into the ground. What with him having no formal training and a lackadaisical work ethic, the business was barely hanging on. Responsibility wasn't in her father's vocabulary. She'd found he would rather take a day off and head to the lake with a fishing pole and a cooler of beer than finish painting projects. So after graduating with a degree in marketing, Logan spurned the high-paying job that couldn't hold her interest and decided to "hang out" with her father for a year or so to see if she could put her education to work.

That was seven years ago. The small business her grandfather had started—painting houses—had thrived and developed into one of the most respected professional painting firms in Austin. Having secured contracts with several of the big builders in town, she'd grown their business from three workers—herself, Ted and Juan—to four teams. They now employed nearly thirty people, and even though she ran the business part of things, she still enjoyed going out with a team from time to time and wielding a paintbrush. She also still liked hanging out with her father at the lake with a cooler of beer.

"Are you still contemplating a new position with Water's Edge?" Logan asked, referring to the company that owned the Rainbow Island Resort.

"I don't know. I love it here. It's close to Mom and Dad. It's close to you," Emma said. "I don't really want to relocate."

"I'd prefer you stay here too," Logan said. "The perks for me are great."

Emma laughed. "Yes, you are quite spoiled, aren't you? Your mother seems to think I should take it, though."

"Why?"

"Because it would be at the corporate level and more money," Emma said. "The last time I had dinner with them, she insinuated I was wasting my skills by managing the resort."

"Yeah. Just like I'm wasting mine by running a painting firm. In her eyes, you're only in a successful career if you're at a desk with a computer, in some damn cubicle."

Emma laughed as her gaze went out to the pool. "Yeah. I much prefer this cubicle." She sat down behind her desk again. "I'm fairly certain I'll turn them down." She paused. "I've met someone."

Logan grinned. "Really? That's great. When do I get to meet her?"

"We'll have dinner one night this week. She lives in Corpus," Emma said. Her phone rang and she glanced at it. "I guess I should get to work. Come by my place tonight. We'll do an early birthday for you. I'll order seafood," she offered as she picked up the phone.

Logan nodded and waved goodbye, her gaze venturing out the window and landing on an enticing pair of tan legs. She decided to ignore Emma's rule about her hitting on the guests. This woman she just had to meet.

CHAPTER THREE

Peyton sipped her drink, a blue frozen concoction that was sweet and refreshing. She sighed contentedly as she watched two women frolicking in the pool. For the first time in months, she was actually relaxing.

She'd even done what Susan had suggested—turn off her phone. Well, not exactly. She couldn't bring herself to actually turn it off, but she did leave it in her room. There could be an emergency, she reasoned. But really, she wasn't worried about the office. She employed two accountants and Susan. She trusted all of them implicitly but especially Susan. She knew Susan would keep things running smoothly in her absence. She planned to check in with them occasionally, that was all. Other than that, she would try her best to put the office from her mind. She was here to relax and recharge, as Susan had said. She intended to do just that.

"You're going to burn if you're not careful."

Peyton had been so lost in thought she hadn't heard the woman approach. She turned her head, finding an attractive young woman watching her with a lazy smile. She held up a bottle of lotion.

"Sunscreen," the woman said. "I highly recommend this brand." Another smile. "And I'll even volunteer my services if you can't reach everything. You know, your back, for instance."

While being shocked by the woman's boldness, Peyton smiled nonetheless. It had been far too many years since someone this young and attractive had flirted with her. Even so, she wasn't really tempted to play along.

"I'm fine. Thank you, though," she said politely. She turned away, hoping the woman would leave.

"I know it's not quite June yet, but you can't be too careful. I'm Logan, by the way."

Peyton turned back to her, trying to estimate her age. Late twenties, she guessed. She had an infectious smile and a hairstyle that was just short and messy enough to leave you wanting to brush it away from her face. She was glad her sunglasses hid her expression; she was shocked by her thoughts.

"Peyton," she said.

To her surprise, the woman pulled a lounge chair close and plopped down, still holding the lotion. Peyton noted that the woman was wearing shorts and a T-shirt and wondered if there was a swimsuit on beneath her clothes. Everyone else in the pool area was dressed appropriately.

"Peyton. I like it. Are you here for the week?"

Peyton blew out her breath. "While I'm flattered by your attention, I'm really not interested," she said bluntly, hoping the woman would get the hint.

But the woman tilted her head, looking bemused. "Interested in what? The lotion?"

Now feeling completely embarrassed, she turned away. Great. She couldn't even discern flirting from normal conversation. She *really* needed to get out more.

"So? The week?" The woman—Logan—asked again. "I'm supposed to be here until Saturday," she volunteered.

Peyton wondered how rude it would be if she simply told the woman to leave, that she wanted to be alone. She shoved her sunglasses on top of her head, intending to do just that. But one look into eyes that were too light to be considered brown, too dark to be considered hazel simply stole her breath away. In fact, she couldn't even remember what she'd been about to say. The words that fell out certainly weren't it.

"How old are you?"

Logan laughed. "For future reference, that's not a great opening line."

Peyton dropped her sunglasses back over her eyes, hoping to hide her embarrassment. "Forget I asked," she mumbled.

"It's okay. I actually have a birthday this week. Thirty."

"Oh? You said that pretty easily. Most women cringe at the thought of turning thirty and try to hold on to twenty-nine as long as possible."

"No, I'm good. Age doesn't mean anything really. It's just a number," she said easily. "I'm comfortable with who I am and where I am in life." She tilted her head again. "I'm going to guess you're…oh, I don't know…forty."

Peyton actually gasped. "Forty? *Forty?*" God, did she look *forty*?

Logan laughed. "Just kidding. I see age does mean something to you."

Peyton smiled, playing along with her. "Yes. And for future reference, that's not a great opening line." She lightly cleared her throat, feeling the need to share her age for fear Logan really did think she was forty. "I'm thirty-four. Birthday in about a month."

"Well, when you and I celebrate my birthday later this week, we'll include a toast for you too."

Peyton raised her eyebrows. "You think we'll celebrate together? Are you always this forward?"

"Only with women whose legs look like yours."

Peyton blushed freely now, feeling a bit out of her element. Such unabashed attention—she was not used to it. She was trying to think of a polite way to ask the woman to leave her in peace when someone called Logan's name.

It was Emma, the woman who had checked her in earlier. Logan turned to Peyton, giving her an apologetic smile.

"I guess my room's ready. Enjoy your sunning." Logan gave her a cute smile and gently slipped the lotion between her thighs.

Peyton was shocked by the thrill she got from such a simple, yet brazen act. "I'll see you later," Logan said with a wink.

Peyton watched her walk away, tall and confident, and was stunned to realize her eyes were glued to not only a pair of long legs but a very nice butt. She pulled her gaze away, quickly snatching up her drink and sucking a generous amount through the straw.

Yes, she *really* needed to get out more.

CHAPTER FOUR

Logan eyed the last shrimp, then glanced at Emma for permission.

"Take it," Emma said with a laugh. "I'd forgotten your obsession with shrimp."

"It's only an obsession when I'm down here at the coast," she said as she bit into the fried shrimp. "Where did you order dinner from? It was excellent."

"Paradise Bar and Grill. They opened up a couple of months ago," Emma said. "Actually, that's where I met Natalie," she said with a smile. "So I have an extra fondness for their food."

"So blind date or what?"

"You know I don't do blind dates," Emma said as she reached over and refilled Logan's wineglass with the crisp, white Gewürztraminer that she loved. "You know my friend Fran, right?"

"Yes," she said as she took a taste of the wine.

"Well, her partner's sister was visiting. So they wanted to do a group dinner. Turns out Natalie is friends with her sister." Emma grinned. "Natalie was actually there with a date, but we hit it off immediately. She got my number from Fran and called me two days later."

"So you like her, huh?"

"I like her a lot. I can't wait for you to meet her."

"I take it she's not still dating this other woman?"

Emma shook her head. "That was their first and last date." She leaned her elbows on the table. "I really, really like her."

Logan noted the wistful look in her eyes, something she'd not seen before. Could her sister finally be in love? Emma was attractive but usually had the worst luck with women. Logan used to tell her she had the worst *taste* in women. She usually fell for those with baggage and drama. It would be nice if she finally found a keeper.

"So what about you? Are you still dating that volleyball player?"

Logan shook her head. "No. Remember? She graduated in December."

"I can't believe you're still dating college-age girls," Emma said with a laugh. "What do they see in you?"

Logan grinned. "It's my charm, baby. But I hated to see her go. She moved to California, trying to hook up with the beach volleyball scene," she said. Her own eyes turned wistful as she pictured Britney in a bikini. "Man, what a body," she said.

"Speaking of bodies, I saw you talking to that woman out by the pool," Emma said.

"Oh, yeah. She's a cutie. She had the prettiest blue eyes I've ever seen. Sky blue. I wanted to just fall in," she admitted. But Peyton had covered those baby blues with her sunglasses again, hiding them. "She's intriguing. Not my normal type. She's almost thirty-five."

"Please don't harass my guests," Emma said with a smile.

"I may have flirted with her a bit. I guess I should find out if she's single, huh?"

"She came alone. Of course that doesn't mean anything."

"So where's she from?"

But Emma shook her head. "You'll have to find out from her. You know I'm a stickler for our privacy policy." She picked up her glass and touched it to Logan's. "So how does it feel to be thirty?"

"I'll tell you in two days," Logan said. "But you should know," she teased.

"Turning thirty was traumatic for me, as you probably remember. You won't have that problem. You couldn't care less how old you are."

Logan shrugged. "Just a number. Just another day."

"Even when we were kids you never really cared much about birthdays," Emma reminded her. "You were more interested in the chocolate cake than your presents. I think you detested the parties."

"I get that from my dad, I think. He's always been so laid-back, a free spirit," she said. "Ted has always lived life the way he wanted. He didn't care what the norm was, what the rules were, what was acceptable." She shrugged. "Of course, those are the same traits that made Mom divorce him."

"Maybe that's why you've always been closer to your dad than Mom," Emma said.

"She favored you anyway," Logan said. "I was too much of a tomboy for her tastes."

Emma laughed. "I did like playing dress up. And even though I wasn't her natural daughter, I think she was more upset that I was gay than she was with you," she said.

"Yes, she took my coming out in stride, didn't she? But you? It might have helped if you hadn't had on a pretty dress when you told them," Logan said with a laugh, remembering the sundress that Emma had been wearing.

"God, I was terrified to tell them. And more scared of your mother than I was my dad," she said. Emma squeezed her arm affectionately. "Thanks for coming to my rescue that day."

Logan gave her a smile and nodded. Even though she was younger than Emma, she'd told her mother she was gay two years before Emma had worked up the courage to do so. Emma hid it all through high school and it wasn't until she was in college that she was able to tell them the truth. As she'd said, her mother took the news far harder than she had when Logan had confessed. Disbelief and shock, then tears had rendered Emma on the verge of tears as well. Logan, still in high school, had made some silly joke and had taken Emma away, letting their parents sort it all out alone.

Her mother had always treated Emma like her own daughter. Logan was never jealous of that. She spent most of her summers in Austin with her dad anyway, leaving Emma behind. And when Logan headed off to college, it was to Austin where her relationship with her father grew even stronger. Not to say that she and her mother had a bad—or strained—relationship, but they were never as close as most mothers and daughters were. That was one reason she was thankful that Emma was there growing up. She had taken the pressure off of Logan when it came to her mother.

As they finished the bottle of wine, their conversation drifted to their childhood and they shared memories and laughter as they reminisced. The sisterly bond they shared knew no boundaries, and Logan was reminded again of just how much she loved her, as a sister and as a friend.

CHAPTER FIVE

Peyton closed her eyes and relaxed under the warm rays of the early afternoon sun. While she had briefly contemplated a walk to the beach, she'd nixed that idea in favor of the chaise lounge by the pool. She was still feeling quite lazy, even after sleeping in that morning and lingering over an early lunch. It was warm but still too early to partake of a fruity drink, so she sipped from her water bottle before placing it underneath the chair. She'd almost...*almost*...forgotten about the office, and she tried now to shove those thoughts away. They could handle things, she knew. And if something had come up, Susan would have called.

So she relaxed, arms and legs stretched out, reaching for the sun, enjoying the breeze that blew in from the Gulf. Another fifteen minutes or so and she'd be ready to plunge into the pool to cool off. Her sunglasses shaded her eyes, but even so, she closed them, listening to the muted conversation of two women who were splashing in the water. Another woman sat alone, reading a book. Peyton had seen her yesterday afternoon with an older woman, but she couldn't determine if they were a couple or not.

"I don't see your skin glistening. Does that mean you forgot the lotion again?"

Peyton didn't have to open her eyes to know it was *her*. She wondered if she ignored her if she would just go away.

"I left it with you, if I recall. And again, I'll offer my services if you need help reaching your back."

Peyton slowly rolled her head to the side, finding Logan looking much like she had the day before—shorts, T-shirt and flip-flops. She said the first thing that came to mind.

"Do you not swim?"

Logan tilted her head. "Yes, I love to swim. Why do you ask?"

"Because we're around the pool and you're the only one not wearing a suit."

Logan grinned. "You want to see me in a suit, do you? A little bikini, maybe?"

"I assure you, that's not what I meant," Peyton said. "I simply asked if you swam."

"Yes, but I get my swimming in early. Like at dawn, with the sun just low enough to lighten the sky. Daybreak. It's a great way to bring on the day," Logan said. A mischievous grin slashed across her face. "But I use the other pool. You know, the one that's clothing optional." Her voice lowered. "You know, no clothing. That means naked."

"I know what clothing optional means," Peyton said dryly. She felt herself blushing and was thankful for her sunglasses.

"Yeah, so I don't know if you're into skinny-dipping or not, but it's the most wonderful thing in the world."

"Not really my thing," she said.

"No? You can join me tomorrow morning," Logan offered. "You could try it out. You might love it."

Peyton shook her head. "Look, I'm flattered by your attention. Really. But I'm not interested," she said frankly.

The smile never left Logan's face. "I thought it was the lotion you weren't interested in."

Peyton couldn't stop the smile that lit her own face as she recalled their conversation from yesterday. "Yes, that too. And no offense, but you're not my type."

"Really?" Logan studied her, her gaze traveling slowly over her body, making Peyton a tad uncomfortable. "Let me guess," Logan continued. "Your type is a little more reserved? Conservative? Professional?"

Peyton didn't answer, but Logan's description was very accurate. And it made her sound so very boring.

"And if my assumption is correct, then yeah, those three things don't describe me at all. I guess I'm really not your type."

"That's correct."

Logan tilted her head, a smile playing on her face. "The obvious solution is…you need a different type."

Again, Logan's smile was infectious and Peyton found herself returning it.

"But speaking of that, I haven't even asked. Are you in a relationship?"

"No," Peyton said. "Actually, at the moment, I hate women."

Logan laughed heartily, loud enough for the woman reading her book to look up sharply. "Bad breakup?"

"It was a bad breakup nine months ago," she said.

"Nine months? And you're still not over her?"

"I'm *so* over her. It's the fact that I caught her in bed with my best friend that I'm not over."

"Ouch."

"Yes. So you see, it's not just you. I hate all women."

As she'd done yesterday, Logan pulled a lounger closer and sat down, swinging her legs up and stretching out. Peyton assumed that meant she wasn't planning on leaving any time soon.

"So you want to talk about it?"

Peyton frowned. "Talk about what?"

"You know, this awful, awful person who's made you hate women."

Peyton laughed. "You want to talk about Vicky?"

"How long were you together?" Logan asked.

"A little over five years," she said. "But I really don't want to talk about her."

"Well, she was obviously crazy. No way would a sane person cheat on you."

Even though Peyton's sunglasses separated them, she could still feel the tug of this attractive young woman. She finally pulled her gaze away, wondering how to respond. She was shocked by the words that spilled from her mouth.

"I don't think I liked her very much anyway."

"Your best friend?"

"No. Vicky." Peyton turned to her. "How does that happen? How do you find yourself in a relationship with someone—for five years, no less—and not really like them?"

"Are you just now realizing you didn't like her?"

"Yes. Well, not right this minute, no." She leaned her head back. "I knew things were strained between us, but I ignored it. She's a chef, so she worked nights."

"A chef? I didn't see that coming," Logan said.

"She's very talented, works at a high-end restaurant, but the last few years, we only saw each other in passing." She reached for her water bottle. "I'm an accountant."

Logan groaned. "God, and I didn't see that coming."

"What's wrong with my profession?"

"Nothing, just…" Logan paused. "You are *so* not my type."

"Well, I'm glad we finally have that established," she said. "Maybe now you'll stop trying to rub lotion on my back."

"I said you weren't my type," Logan said. "I didn't say I would stop flirting with you."

"Then you're wasting your time. Really."

"It's hardly a waste, Peyton. Your body is, well, it's perfect. From what I can see of it."

Peyton felt herself blushing yet again and had to stop herself from grabbing her towel and covering herself. She was proud of her body and didn't mind the compliment, but something about the way Logan looked at her caused her to…well, caused her to feel heated.

"I'm glad you approve," she managed, keeping her gaze on the pool and not on the annoyingly attractive woman flirting with her.

"That skinny-dipping offer is still on the table," Logan continued. "I'll be able to give you a better assessment of your body then."

Peyton laughed. "Do you ever give up?"

"Well, if you called the police, I would probably have to."

"Don't tempt me."

"Am I tempting you? Good. Then we're making progress," Logan teased.

But Peyton shook her head as she laughed. "I told you, you're wasting your time on me."

"Well, there are worse things," Logan said. "But I guess I should leave you in peace. I've got some errands to do before my dinner date."

"Oh? Did someone fall for your charm?"

"No. Sadly, it's with a couple. I'll be the third wheel. Unless you want to join me," Logan offered.

"No, no. Thank you though. You have fun."

Logan sat up and leaned closer, touching Peyton's thigh with the tip of her index finger. Peyton actually felt a tremor run through her.

"Don't get too much sun," Logan said quietly. Then she winked. "I'll think about you tonight."

Before Peyton could respond, she was gone, walking away in a confident walk that Peyton was beginning to recognize. God, but she's cute, Peyton admitted. And she had a pleasant sense of humor, if you liked that sort of thing. Which, of course, Peyton didn't. She was used to reserved, conservative and professional. And boring. She guessed time spent with Logan would be anything but boring.

She sighed. Didn't matter. She was here to relax and recharge, nothing more.

"Excuse me."

Peyton shoved her sunglasses on top of her head, eyeing, not the waitress from the bar, but the icy glass she held.

"I didn't order a drink," Peyton said.

"No, it's from your friend. She asked me to bring it over."

Peyton stared at the orangey red drink. "What is it?"

"It's a Sex on the Beach."

"Of course it is," she murmured with a smile. She nodded her thanks, waiting until the waitress was gone before taking a sip. It was strong and delicious and refreshing, and it gave her a tingling feeling all the way down to her toes. "Sex on the Beach, indeed," she said as she sucked on the straw again.

CHAPTER SIX

Logan paced in her room, wondering if she dared go through with her somewhat crazy plan. On the one hand, it sounded fun. And kinda romantic. Not that Peyton had given any indication that she was looking for something romantic. Quite the contrary, in fact. Which, in turn, intrigued her more. Why was Peyton being so standoffish? She's single, she's at a lesbian resort, she's on vacation. Sure, Peyton hates all women at the moment, but that didn't mean *her*, did it? Because, Logan admitted, she was quite captivated by her. It didn't hurt that her first two encounters were with Peyton in a bikini. She closed her eyes, picturing those smooth, tan legs, the curve of her hip, the swell of her breasts. *Damn*. It had been awhile since she had been this physically attracted to someone. Well, the volleyball player notwithstanding.

But then, Peyton was an accountant. And she appeared to be a bit uptight. And her tastes ran quite the opposite of what Logan was. Of course, Logan's tastes did too.

"Well, I don't want to marry her," she murmured. She just wanted to get to know her—and her body—a little better. She saw nothing wrong with a little vacation fling. It would be fun.

Of course, there was Emma. Emma, who had finally given up Peyton's room number despite it "breaking every privacy policy in the book," had made Logan promise that she wasn't stalking her. And she wasn't. She would simply go to her room, make a suggestion for a walk on the beach and mind her manners. And if Peyton asked her to leave, she would. Yes, of course she would. It wasn't like she would resort to begging.

But damn, she was cute. And she had those killer blue eyes. And that body.

"Maybe I would beg a little," she said to the empty room. Then she laughed. "But I'm not a stalker."

She took the stairs up to the second floor, not trusting the rickety elevator, even though Emma assured her it was perfectly safe. She walked quietly down the empty hallway, pausing at Room 122.

"God, I hope she doesn't get pissed."

* * *

Peyton opened her eyes, hearing faint knocking. She rolled over, assuming it was another room. The knocking got louder. She opened her eyes again, fumbling for her phone.

"Eleven thirty?" She rolled over and pounded her pillow with a sigh, only to throw the covers off as the knocking got louder. She marched to the door and jerked it open. "What?"

"Good. You're still up."

Peyton stared in disbelief, then gave her best scowl. "You? Really? *You?*"

Logan nodded. "Yeah. You remember me, right? Logan. We chatted by the pool earlier." She grinned. "You had Sex on the Beach."

Peyton rolled her eyes at Logan's reference to her drink. "There'd better be a fire. It's the middle of the night and you're knocking on my door. So there'd better be a fire."

Logan shook her head. "First, it's not the middle of the night. And secondly, if there was a fire, you'd hear women screaming and running down the hallway. Maybe hear sirens already too." She stepped back and made a show of looking in both directions. "No fire."

"Then *what* could you possibly be doing here?"

Logan tapped an imaginary watch on her wrist. "Hurry up. Get dressed."

"What? It's the middle of the night. I'm not getting dressed."

"It's not the middle of the night. It's not even midnight," Logan said.

"When you've been in bed since nine-thirty, it's the middle of the freakin' night," Peyton said with a bit of impatience. The woman was annoying. Whatever in the world made her think she was cute? "I want to go back to sleep."

"Good God! You went to bed at nine thirty? I thought you were on vacation. Peyton, really, you're acting like you're, you know, forty or something."

Peyton stared at her. "I'm not even going to reply to that. Good night," she said, intending to close the door. She wasn't surprised to find a hand blocking her.

"Come on. Put some shorts on. Time's a wasting," Logan said.

It was only then that Peyton realized her lack of attire. She was horrified that she was standing at the door in nothing but her underwear and a sleep shirt. She immediately pulled the shirt down to cover her underwear, knowing how ridiculous she was being. Logan had already seen her in a bikini.

"What...are you doing here?"

"The moon. The midnight moon. The sun and the moon are aligned. The tide will be exceptional, but we've got to hurry."

Peyton's patience was slipping. "What are you talking about?"

"We're going to the beach. Come on. It'll be fun."

"*What?* No."

"Yes. It's a full moon tonight. Midnight, it'll be over the beach, over the water. It'll be fantastic."

Peyton stared at her, slowly shaking her head. "Are you serious? You woke me up for that? Because I'm fairly certain I've seen a full moon before."

"But, Peyton, not this one."

The words were spoken so quietly, so softly, that Peyton had no retort. Maybe it was the way Logan said her name that left her speechless. So she simply walked back into her room and grabbed the shorts she'd discarded earlier that evening. Apparently she was going to the beach to look at a full moon.

CHAPTER SEVEN

Logan brought a finger to her lips. "We've got to be quiet," she whispered as they headed to the stairs. "It's the middle of the night. People are trying to sleep." She grinned when she heard Peyton nearly giggle at her comment. Okay, so maybe she wasn't pissed after all. "Oh, and I'm really not a stalker," she added.

"That's reassuring," Peyton said.

Logan had stashed a couple of blankets—and a bottle of wine—out by the pool. She hadn't wanted to seem too presumptuous when she'd knocked on her door. And while she'd opened the bottle of wine so she didn't have to carry a corkscrew, she'd failed to think of glasses. Not too romantic drinking right out of the bottle. Even *she* wouldn't do that. Well, in a pinch, maybe.

"A blanket?"

"Just to sit on," Logan said. "No hanky-panky." She handed Peyton the wine. "Promise."

Peyton held up the bottle to the light. "Nice choice."

"Thank you. I stole it from the office. I'm not really an expert on wine. Glad you approve."

"It's a nice bottle. There'll still be no hanky-panky."

"Why would you even think that?" Logan said innocently. "I enjoy your company. It's not like I want to ravish your body." She paused. "Much."

Peyton laughed. "Are you always so forward?"

"I'm only here four more days. I have to work fast."

"Wait a minute. You *stole* it?"

Logan laughed. "I can explain. Later."

As soon as they left the muted lighting of the pool area and walked on the boardwalk across the dunes, Logan casually took her hand. "Don't want you to trip," she said with a smile. She was surprised that Peyton didn't pull her hand away.

As soon as they hit the beach, she knew her crack at seduction had gotten a bit easier. The full moon was absolutely beautiful. The white orb engulfed the sky, its light dancing across the waves as they crashed on shore. The few scattering of clouds only enhanced the show. She turned, finding Peyton staring out over the water, the breeze blowing her hair back from her face, the glow of the moon bright enough for her to make out each and every feature of Peyton's face. She was nearly mesmerized as Peyton turned, meeting her eyes in the glimmering moonlight. Peyton smiled slightly, her blue eyes still holding hers.

"It's gorgeous."

Logan nodded, feeling seduced herself. "Yes, gorgeous." She felt her heart beat just a little too fast as their stare continued. Damn, but she wanted to kiss her already. Before she could do just that, Peyton turned away, breaking the spell.

So Logan did the sensible thing. She walked a little farther down the beach, looking for a spot to sit. It was a very high tide with the moon overhead so she tossed out the blanket closer to the sand dunes, away from the lapping water. The breeze flipped the edges of the blanket up and she smoothed them back down. She sat, motioning for Peyton to do the same. She took the wine bottle from her, balanced it between her legs and leaned back on her elbows.

"I love this," she said. "The midnight moon. It looks so big, it's almost like you could reach out and touch it."

"Yes." Peyton tucked a stray strand of hair behind her ear. "Thanks for making me do this," she said. "I've never...well, I've seen the full moon, of course, but usually it's when I'm driving. I don't think I've ever intentionally gone outside to look at it."

"A lot of people don't. But I feel like we should celebrate the wonders of our earth, our existence. People are always in such a hurry, rushing around from place to place. They don't take the time to really appreciate the things around them." She sat up and pulled the cork out of the wine bottle. "I get that from my father. He's so laid-back, nothing stresses him out. He could sit and stare at the lake all day long. Well, as long as he was fishing." She twirled the cork between her fingers. "I kinda forgot the glasses."

Peyton surprised her by taking the bottle from her and bringing it up to her mouth for a drink. She handed it back to Logan with a nod.

"Very nice." Peyton smiled. "And no, I've never had wine straight out of the bottle before."

"Well, you're living on the edge tonight."

Logan followed suit, taking a sip, then another. She felt no need for conversation and they sat quietly, watching the light change on the water as each wave rushed to shore. It was a pleasant night, the breeze not too strong, but she laid out the other blanket across their legs. Peyton said nothing, just continued to stare out over the water. The wine bottle got passed back and forth in silence a few times. Logan finally corked it again when Peyton leaned back, crossing her arms behind her head, her gaze traveling up to the moon. Logan lay back too, resting comfortably beside Peyton. The sights and sounds were hypnotic as she watched the moon slowly crawl across the night sky. She quickly lost track of time. Without even realizing it, the rhythmic sound of the tide was lulling her to sleep. She turned her head, about to suggest to Peyton that they head back. But Peyton was fast asleep beside her, her face relaxed and peaceful.

"My God, she's pretty," Logan whispered, her words carried away in the breeze.

So instead of waking her, she pulled the blanket up a little higher and covered them both, thinking she'd stay out just a little longer. Unfortunately, the peacefulness that surrounded her—and the presence of a very warm body next to her—quieted all her senses and her eyes slipped closed too. She gave in to the relaxed state of her body and mind and drifted off to sleep, still clinging to the notion that she would rest for only a few more minutes.

The hoarse croak of a heron roused her, and she was shocked to find the soft white glow of the moon replaced with the subtle pink and red of a rapidly rising sun. She rolled to her side, intending to wake Peyton, but the heron was only fifteen feet away, creeping slowly along the beach. His silhouette was a perfect backdrop to the lightening sky. She wished she had a camera.

Peyton must have sensed her watching. Her eyes fluttered opened, confusion shadowing them.

"Don't move," Logan whispered. "You'll scare him."

"Him who?"

"The heron."

Peyton rolled her head to the side. "It's *dawn*?" she asked, surprise in her voice.

"Yeah. So now we're forced to watch the sunrise. How cool is that?"

Peyton rolled her head back toward Logan. "We *slept* out here? We could have been mugged or something."

"Mugged? Out here? What are they going to take? The wine?"

"You know what I mean."

The heron took flight, his long legs pushing off the sand, and he landed a safer distance away from them.

"Actually, I stayed awake the whole night, making sure you were safe," Logan said. "I'm gallant that way."

Peyton stretched. "Really? Then why are your eyes all sleepy looking?"

"I may have napped a little." Logan sat up and reached for Peyton, pulling her into a sitting position as well. "But look at it this way, you'll get to see a beautiful sunrise without me beating on your door to wake you."

"I have to pee."

Logan nodded. "Yeah, so do I."

Peyton turned to her and slowly shook her head. "I don't even know you, and I spent the night sharing a blanket on the beach."

"I told you it'd be fun."

"You're missing the point," Peyton said.

"The point is, we saw a beautiful moon, beautiful colors. It was a perfect night. And now, because *one* of us fell asleep, we get to see a gorgeous sunrise. In fact, you may like it so much, you'll want to come out here every morning." Logan smiled. "Of course, this is normally when I get my skinny-dipping in."

"Well, don't let me stop you."

"No? You ready to join me?"

"I'm ready for a bathroom, a shower and a cup of coffee," she said as her gaze drifted back over the water. "Look how far out the tide is compared to last night."

Logan nodded. "When I was five, my mother remarried and we moved to Corpus. We used to go out to the beach all the time when I was growing up. We had this chart at the house where we tracked the tides. The tide is always very high when there's a full moon overhead," she said. "Like last night. I don't remember all the facts, but I think it takes like six hours or so to go from high tide to low tide."

"So you grew up down here?"

"Well, Corpus. But we came to the island all the time." She pointed. "Here comes the sun."

"The clouds make it really pretty."

"Yeah. I always wished I'd gotten into photography," she said. She pulled her cell phone out of her pocket. "This is about the extent of it." She held up the phone, snapping a couple of pictures as the sun rose out of the water.

"Okay, I'll confess. I've never actually seen a real live sunrise before," Peyton said. "It's kinda refreshing to be out here at this hour. It's so quiet."

Logan didn't say anything as her eyes followed the progress of the reddish orange ball that shimmered across the surface, reflecting its colors on the high clouds overhead. Then, as if a breakfast bell had sounded, gulls and terns flew over the surf with their familiar calls and pelicans circled and dove into the water, looking for food. A new day had begun.

"Thank you."

Logan turned, finding Peyton's blue eyes on her. She simply nodded and stood up, stretching her back by holding her arms overhead. She held out a hand to Peyton, who let herself be pulled up. Silently, they each took a blanket and headed back. Logan's gaze went to the smooth sand where the tide had ironed it flat. She spotted a sand dollar and went to pick it up.

"You don't usually find them intact," she said, holding it out to Peyton.

Peyton took it, turning it over gently in her hands.

"You keep it," Logan said. "A memento of your first midnight moon."

Peyton rolled her eyes slightly but folded her hand around the sand dollar as they headed over the dunes and back to the boardwalk.

"I'll walk you up to your room," Logan offered as they got to the hotel.

"That's not necessary."

"I insist," she said. "We'll even use the elevator. It's old. Very old." She grinned as the doors closed. "Maybe we'll get stranded."

But the old hulk of a lift made it to the second floor without incident. Logan held the door as she motioned for Peyton to exit. She was about to follow when Peyton spun around.

"Wait a minute," Peyton said. "How did you know which room was mine?"

Logan bit her lower lip. *Damn.* "Lucky guess?" she said weakly.

Peyton tilted her head with raised eyebrows. "Try again."

The elevator doors tried to push closed and Logan stepped back inside. "Okay, so maybe I am stalking you. Maybe I've been following you. You should be more careful of strangers." She grinned and gave an exaggerated wink as the doors closed.

Her smile vanished as the elevator lurched. Emma was going to kill her.

CHAPTER EIGHT

"You did what?"

"She's not going to file a complaint," Logan insisted. "At least I don't think so." She stole a french fry from Emma's plate. "And it's not like I had planned to stay out there all night."

"Please don't get me fired."

"She's cute."

"Sure. But she's not your type," Emma said.

"Oh, I know. But did you get a good look at her body?"

"I did. That's the only thing about her that *is* your type," Emma said with a laugh.

"Yeah. She doesn't seem the sort for a holiday romance," Logan said. "But I can try. At least it gives me something to do." She ate the last bite of her burger and wadded up the wrapper. "So are you and Natalie going to the shindig down the beach?"

"Over at the Conch Hotel? Matt invited us, yes. When did you talk to him?"

"I went by there yesterday before I met you guys for dinner." She raised her eyebrows. "So you going?"

"Are you?"

Logan shrugged. "It is my birthday today. Matt at least remembered so I suppose I should show up. He's got a 'fabulous new gumbo dish that's to die for,'" she mimicked.

Emma laughed. "He's such a queen. Literally. He's doing drag shows now, did he tell you?"

Logan nodded. Matt Canton was Emma's age and they'd all gone to high school together. He was always flamboyant and never apologized for it. He got picked on in school, of course, but that had never deterred him. Matt was one of the smartest people she knew and could have done anything, but he was too entrenched in the beach scene to leave the area. He'd been working at hotels on the island since he turned eighteen. This was his third year as manager of the Conch. In fact, he's the one who got Emma interested in the business.

"So what are your plans for the afternoon?" Emma asked. "And please don't say you're doing more stalking."

"I'll probably hang out by the pool," she said as she glanced out the window in Emma's office. Peyton had yet to make an appearance. "Maybe walk to the beach and splash around."

"Please behave yourself," Emma warned.

"I'm attracted to her. What can I say?" Logan stood and pushed the visitor chair closer to Emma's desk.

"You can say you won't do anything stupid." Emma tossed the remnants of her burger into the trash. "Thanks for lunch. Maybe we'll see you tonight over at the Conch."

"Yep. Later, sis."

When she'd left Peyton earlier that morning, Logan was still feeling drained and had gone back to her room, intending to take a quick nap on a real bed. It had lasted until ten thirty. After a shower and a late cup of coffee, she was ready to enjoy another day at the beach. But when Peyton was a no-show at the pool, she'd offered to get lunch for Emma. Now, with the afternoon ahead of her, she peeked around the corner of the pool, looking for Peyton in her normal spot. Nothing.

Well, she couldn't go up to Peyton's room. She'd just have to wait her out.

God, I am a stalker.

That thought amused her and she headed in the opposite direction to her corner room, a smile on her face. She stripped out of her shorts and found her bikini, a sleek black one that the volleyball player had gotten for her. Her breasts were small, but Britney had said this suit made them look perky.

"Perky," she muttered with a shake of her head. But then, Britney had been twenty-one. Talk about nothing in common, that was them. But damn, the sex had been good.

Logan stood by the mirror, looking at herself. With her penchant for skinny-dipping, it was a plus to live only a few miles from Drew Montgomery and her spring-fed pool. Logan used it nearly every day. She patted her stomach, noting she wasn't as thin as she used to be. She turned sideways, sighing with relief.

"You're not fat."

No, the bikini fit her nicely. She silently thanked Britney for the gift, not sure if she would care or not that she was using it to seduce another woman. *Attempt* to seduce, she corrected. And time was wasting.

She grabbed a towel and one of the complimentary bottles of lotion. On the way to the pool, she stopped at Emma's office to steal a bottle of cold water from her fridge. Emma was on the phone and only waved at her.

CHAPTER NINE

Peyton was actually disappointed that Logan was nowhere to be found when she settled in her lounge chair. For a Wednesday, the pool was crowded and noisy, making her wish she'd brought her iPod. Instead, she turned on her Kindle and brought up the latest book in the series she'd been hooked on for years. Trying to lose herself in the story, she ignored the laughter and chatter from the women around her, but she couldn't help but to glance up from time to time, hoping for the dark-headed Logan to make an appearance.

Be thankful she's leaving you in peace.

I don't really even like her, she thought. Logan was a bit too...too spontaneous for her. Peyton liked her life organized. She liked having plans and agendas. Like this vacation. Susan had wanted her to dash off the very week she'd told her about Rainbow Island Resort. It had taken nearly a month of planning and shuffling her schedule around before she felt comfortable enough to make the reservations. Of course, she was glad she finally had. She was relaxing. She was recharging. She was actually having fun.

Well, she'd had fun last night. After she got over the initial shock of someone pounding on her door in the middle of the night, that is.

She looked up now, just in time to see a familiar face heading her way. She tried not to stare but *Jesus*, Logan looked good in a bikini. Thankful that her eyes were shaded by her sunglasses, she made a show of staring at her book.

"Like I didn't see you looking," Logan said with an easy smile. She pulled a chair closer and plopped down.

"Looking at what?"

"Oh, please." Logan leaned closer. "What are you reading? One of those lesbian romance books with lots of hot sex?"

Peyton shook her head. "Kay Scarpetta."

"I've read a few of those," Logan said. "But...the day's a-wasting." She swung her long legs off of the lounger and got up as quickly as she'd sat down. "Let's go to the beach."

"I don't think so," Peyton said, holding up her Kindle.

"Come on, it'll be fun." From under her towel Logan produced a Frisbee. "We'll play."

"Frisbee?" Peyton shook her head. "I don't remember the last time I've thrown one. I'm not sure I know how."

"So we'll play."

Peyton hesitated. It would be fun, playing on the beach. But she wasn't a beach person, she reminded herself. But seeing Logan standing there in next to nothing, her body lean and tan, made her want to become a beach person.

God, whatever in the world is wrong with me?

"Come on. It's my birthday. Spend it with me."

How could she say no to that? God, what was it about this woman that pulled her out of her element so easily? She turned off her Kindle and slipped it into her bag, aware of the triumphant smile on Logan's face as she nodded.

"Great. Grab a couple of towels."

Peyton did and followed Logan away from the pool and to the boardwalk, much as they'd done last night. The beach was not very crowded, but there were people about. Logan led them down a ways, finding a spot all to themselves.

"Once schools are out for summer, the beach gets crazy," Logan said. "I try to stay away then."

"Is this where you used to come when you were young?"

"Sometimes. But Padre Island National Seashore is closer to Corpus, so we'd go there mostly. Or to the state park—Mustang Island."

Logan laid out her towel, and Peyton did the same, keeping some space between them. All Logan had brought with her was the Frisbee and a bottle of water. And, of course, lotion. Logan saw her glance at it and she held it up.

"Need me to put some on your back? Don't want you to burn, you know."

"Do you have a lotion fetish?"

Logan gave her a flirty grin. "No. I have an 'I want to touch your soft skin' fetish."

Peyton laughed but shook her head at the lotion. "I'm good for now."

"Well, come on then. Let's get wet."

Logan took off in a slow jog toward the water, Frisbee in hand. Peyton hesitated. There were probably all sorts of...of *things* in the water. Jellyfish, for one.

"Come on, Peyton," Logan called as she was already in the water. "It'll be fun."

It's the bikini, she told herself. That's the *only* reason she was doing this. So she headed in Logan's direction, pausing when her bare feet touched the water. It was cooler than she'd imagined, but she walked in up to her knees, feeling the pull and push of the waves. She laughed as one caught her waist-high, nearly knocking her over. Logan walked away from her, holding the Frisbee up. Peyton nodded, wondering if she even remembered how to catch the damn thing. But Logan tossed it softly, and Peyton snatched it out of the air. Logan cheered as if Peyton had made a touchdown.

"I can't throw it," she warned.

"Give it a try."

She did. It sailed high and to the right, landing on the beach. Logan jogged after it, and Peyton was left staring at her as she ran.

"Here you go," Logan called, tossing it again.

This one was a little harder but right to her. Peyton used both hands to secure it. She bent down just a bit to throw, trying to get some spin on the disc. This one was much better and Logan ran into the surf to catch it. Again, Peyton stared, her eyes glued to what little the bikini covered.

They tossed it back and forth, both of them soaking wet as they ran in the water. Peyton couldn't remember the last time she'd played like that. She was having more fun than she'd had in years.

Logan finally called an end to their game, tossing the Frisbee up near their towels before diving into the surf. Peyton watched her as she swam out a little way, letting the waves carry her back in, then going out again. It looked like fun and Peyton was feeling adventurous. So off she went, hopping over the first two waves until she was waist deep, then diving under water much as Logan had done. She was a strong swimmer—she swam nearly daily in her pool when the weather allowed—but the Gulf was altogether different. When she got out to where she wasn't touching bottom, she almost panicked. But Logan swam near her, smiling reassuringly.

"It's okay. Let's ride it in," Logan said.

She relaxed, taking her offered hand, and they paddled back toward shore. She felt relief when her feet touched bottom again. She walked out of the water, slicking her hair back from her face and smiling into the sun.

"God, what fun," she said.

"Sure was," Logan agreed as she plopped down on her towel, arms stretched out to her sides.

Peyton tried not to stare as she dropped to her own towel. She didn't know what was wrong with her. It's not like she hadn't seen a woman in a bikini before. In fact, several up at the pool were wearing bikinis. Although, she had to admit, not a one of them came close to filling it out quite like Logan did.

"So an accountant, huh?"

Peyton rolled her head to the side. "Yes."

"So where are you from?"

Peyton smiled. "You may possibly be a stalker. Do you actually think I'm going to tell you where I live?"

Logan smiled too. "Fair enough."

Peyton intended to just lie still and enjoy the sun, but her curiosity got the better of her. "What about you?"

"What about me?"

"What do you do? When you're not stalking women," she added and Logan laughed.

"I'm a painter."

"A painter? Like an artist?"

"No, no. A painter. You know, bucket of paint, paintbrush, houses, walls and stuff."

"Oh." Peyton wasn't sure what she expected but a…a painter wasn't it. She could honestly say that she'd never ever been out with a painter before. Of course, it wasn't like this was a date or anything. But still. A painter. Okay, so she was judging. She admitted it. She was used to professional women. Not…laborers. She turned her head away, embarrassed by her thoughts.

I did not just think that, did I?

Yes, she did and she felt terrible about it. There was nothing wrong with being a painter. She was about to apologize to Logan for her thoughts when Logan sat up.

"Okay, look, there's nothing sexual about this at all," she said, holding up the sunscreen. "But you're starting to burn. Let me just slap some on your back. You won't even have time to get aroused."

Peyton arched an eyebrow at her. "Aroused? As if you rubbing lotion on my skin would arouse me."

Logan gave her what could only be described as a sexy smile. "Don't tempt me to prove otherwise."

Their stare was intense, and Peyton finally accepted the challenge. Her skin did feel hot, but she wasn't sure if it was from the sun or Logan's dare.

"I suppose I am a little…warm."

Again, that sexy smile. "You're way past warm, Peyton. You're hot. Very hot."

Peyton laughed. "God, where do you come up with these lines?"

Logan grinned. "What? Too much?"

"Yes."

Logan motioned with her finger. "Turn around."

Peyton did as she was told, waiting while Logan squirted lotion into her palm. She closed her eyes when Logan touched her, her hand sliding smoothly across her shoulders and upper back. She could feel the heat of her skin and the lotion did feel good, she admitted. Of course, she wasn't sure if it was the lotion that felt good or simply Logan's soft hands touching her.

"Now turn this way."

Peyton did, watching as Logan's lotion-coated fingers rubbed her upper arms.

"See, nothing sensual about this," Logan said. "But you could have reached this yourself, I guess."

Peyton was about to reply when Logan's fingers lightly brushed the side of her breast. Logan stopped instantly and their eyes met.

"I swear, that was an accident," Logan said.

"Sure it was."

"Really. If it was intentional, I would have done a much better job."

Peyton laughed. "It's okay."

Logan reached out and rubbed her nose with the remaining lotion on her fingers. "Don't want it to burn."

With their eyes still locked together, the words that left Peyton's mouth were spoken well before she had time to consider them.

"Would you like me to do your back?"

"Honey, I'd like you to do a lot more than just my back," Logan said with a saucy grin. Then, "Oh, you mean the lotion? That would be great too."

Peyton told herself they were just playing, teasing. Nothing more. So she scooted closer, putting a generous amount of the sunscreen in her palm. She waited until Logan turned her back to her, then reached out, lightly touching Logan's shoulders, rubbing her hands in gentle circles as she smoothed the lotion on her skin. It shouldn't have felt so good—so sensual—but it did. As her fingers brushed across Logan's smooth skin, it occurred to her that it had been well over a year since she'd touched another woman. She hadn't realized how much she'd missed the intimacy of touching someone.

Of course, there was nothing intimate about this, she reminded herself. She hardly even knew this woman, and they were simply putting lotion on where the other couldn't reach. It wasn't like this was foreplay or anything. Yet her hands continued their ministrations, across Logan's back to her shoulders and upper arms. She was almost mesmerized by it, and she admitted that, yes, she was a little aroused. That thought made her stop her movements, taking her hand away from Logan's shoulder.

"God, that felt good," Logan murmured. "I bet you give great back rubs."

Peyton wiped the remaining lotion on her own legs. "Honestly, I don't think I've ever given a back rub before," she said.

Logan laid on her side, facing Peyton, a smile still on her face. "We could remedy that, you know."

Peyton lay down too but rolled to her back. "Seeing as there's no one in my life to give back rubs to, I don't see the point in practicing," she said lightly.

"Why didn't you ever give…what was her name again?"

"Vicky."

"Yeah, Vicky. She didn't like them?"

"I don't guess it ever came up," she said. She chewed on her lower lip as she thought back to their sex life. It had been good. Satisfying. Yet, toward the end, not so much. She couldn't really pinpoint when it had changed. The last year of their relationship had been…well, rather dry. She blamed it on their schedules. She blamed it on a lot of things. But she never blamed it on them growing apart. That hadn't occurred to her. To this day, she wondered if they'd still be together if she hadn't caught Vicky in bed with Alicia.

"Do you still miss her?" Logan asked, her words sincere and not teasing.

Peyton rolled her head to the side and looked at her. "No, not really. At first, I missed having that partner, you know. And I told you she was a chef. I missed her cooking," she said with a smile. "But after it was over, I learned some things about her that I hadn't been able to see when we were together."

"Like what?"

"Like she uses women for a nice place to live and pretends to be in love with them." The words sounded bitter, which she supposed, they should. "Sorry."

"You were together how long? Five years? That's a long time to pretend," Logan said. "On her part, I mean."

"Yes, it is. I guess that's why she was cheating on me. Alicia wasn't the first one. And if I hadn't caught them in bed, I doubt she would have been the last."

"So you kicked her out. Then what?"

"She started dating an attorney, a woman I had once dated. She moved in with her shortly after that."

Logan laughed quietly. "Actually, the 'then what' was meant for you."

"Oh. Well, then nothing. I hate women, remember."

"So you haven't dated?"

"No. And I don't plan to."

"You're only thirty-five. That's too early to give up on dating," Logan said.

"Thirty-four, thank you," Peyton corrected. "And what about you?"

"What about me?"

"Are you single?"

Logan laughed again. "I must be doing a horrible job at flirting if you think I'm involved with someone."

"Well, as my recent experience shows, being involved with someone doesn't matter," she said.

"But I'm not guilty of that," Logan said. "I haven't ever been in a real relationship. I dated in college. And it seems I'm still dating college students. They tend to graduate and move on, though. No time for a relationship."

"So you went to college?"

"Sure."

"Is that where you learned to paint?"

Logan laughed yet again, and Peyton loved the sound of it. "No," was all she said as she too rolled onto her back.

They were quiet, and Peyton listened to the sound of the surf, the gulls, the faraway sounds of laughter coming from others on the beach. She had no idea how long they'd been out, but it was one of the most enjoyable afternoons she'd spent in a long, long time.

"Thank you," she said.

"For what?"

"I had fun today."

Logan nodded. "Yeah, it's fun playing on the beach."

"I can't even begin to tell you the last time I played Frisbee," she said.

"You're pretty good too. When you said you were an accountant, I was afraid you wouldn't even know what a Frisbee was," Logan teased.

Peyton smiled, not taking offense. "Well, you were much better than me. I could tell you are an athlete."

Logan rolled to her side and leaned on her elbow, her eyes dancing with amusement. "As you know, I'm a painter. I'm outside, up and down ladders. And I swim a lot." She wiggled her eyebrows. "Skinny-dipping. I'm very limber and flexible," she continued. "I also play on a softball team." She smiled broadly. "Did I mention I'm flexible?"

Peyton laughed out loud but didn't dare reply.

Logan sat up, still smiling. "I guess on that note, we should wrap it up," she said. "I think I've had enough sun for the day."

Peyton sat up too. "A cold shower sounds nice."

"A cold beer sounds nice," Logan countered.

They shook out their towels, then trudged through the sand back to the boardwalk, making their way to the pool area. Peyton dared to peek into the semiprivate clothing optional pool. Four women were there, two in the pool and two lounging on chairs. The two lounging were topless. She turned away quickly, blushing as Logan gave a light chuckle.

"Want to join them?"

"I do not," Peyton said quickly. She was about to suggest they part company when Logan suggested something else entirely.

"Come out with me this evening."

Peyton raised her eyebrows. "Out?"

"Early dinner. At dusk."

Peyton hesitated. Yes, she'd had a wonderful day and had enjoyed Logan's company immensely. But dinner at dusk sounded like…well, not a normal dress-up dinner at a restaurant. As she'd gotten to know Logan better, she'd learned there wasn't a lot that was *normal* about her. At least, not what Peyton perceived as normal.

"We've already spent most of the day together," she said.

Logan nodded. "Yeah. Wasn't it great?"

Peyton still hesitated. "It's your birthday," she said. "Isn't there someone you'd rather spend it with?"

Logan's smile was slow and, well, sexy. "At this very moment, I can't think of another soul I'd rather spend it with." Then the sexy smile was replaced with a genuine one. "Besides, I hear you have a birthday coming up soon. We should celebrate both."

"We should?"

Logan nodded. "So what do you say? A hotel down the way," she pointed, "is having their weekly seafood extravaganza on the beach for their guests."

Peyton stared blankly at her. "But we're not their guests."

"Oh, I know. We're going to crash it. It'll be fun."

"Um…no," Peyton said with a quick shake of her head. "I'm not crashing another hotel's party. We could get into trouble."

Logan laughed. "We're not going to get into trouble."

"No. I'm not doing it."

Logan stepped closer to her. So close that had she not been holding her towel in front of her their thighs would be brushing. It was an intimate gesture, and she tried not to let Logan know how her closeness was affecting her.

"Don't be afraid to take a chance," Logan said. "You might be surprised at the outcome."

Peyton wasn't sure if they were still talking about dinner or not, but she fell into her eyes—those eyes that were neither brown nor hazel but somewhere in between. She fell in and couldn't drag herself back out.

"Come on, Peyton. It'll be fun."

The softly spoken words, not much more than a whisper, reverberated in her mind.

Take a chance. It'll be fun. Peyton.

Maybe it was the way her name sounded when Logan spoke it, but she seemed powerless to resist her offer. So against her better judgment, she nodded.

"Okay. I'll go with you."

Logan's grin was infectious and Peyton returned it.

"Great! I'll meet you back down here about six thirty," Logan said. She turned to go, then stopped. "It's on the beach. Casual."

Peyton nodded and watched as she walked away. Yes. Casual. Not a normal dinner date with one of the professional—conservative, reserved—friends she normally went out with. She had a contented smile on her face as she made her way to the elevator that would take her up to her room. Logan was so different from anyone she'd ever spent time with, it was refreshing. She was a little bit out of her element—crashing parties wasn't something she'd ever done before. But after a fun day on the beach, she wasn't really ready for their time together to end. That surprised her. Because as she'd told herself many times, Logan wasn't her type. At all.

As the old elevator jerked upward, a slow smile spread across her face. Not her type, no. But she sure looked good in a bikini. She convinced herself that was the *only* reason she was going out with her.

CHAPTER TEN

Logan hadn't intended on a nap. No, she was just going to lay down for a bit and rest. She'd stripped off the bikini and was heading to the shower when she glanced at the bed. The sheets were cool. The AC was turned down low. She didn't stand a chance. She jumped into the shower long enough to rinse the sand off, then fell into bed. But after what seemed like hours later, she sat up with a start, blinking several times to clear her head.

Dinner with Peyton.

She jumped up, grabbing her phone. She let out a sigh of relief. It was only five forty-five.

Never being one to nap, she blamed it on the beach and the sun...and the fun. The last few years, she'd been so busy with the business, she hadn't really taken the time for play. Trips to the lake with her father and hanging out with Drew and Jay at their spring-fed pool were the few highlights lately. Well, not including playing with the volleyball player. But that was an entirely different kind of playing, she noted.

And I'm getting too old to keep that pace, she thought.

"Yeah, turning over a new leaf at thirty," she said with a grin, knowing it was a lie. What was she trying to do with Peyton anyway?

She hurried through her shower, although she did take the time to shave her legs. Not that she was being presumptuous, she told herself. Just because.

She never brought anything with her other than shorts and jeans to wear and this trip was no different. But it was too warm for jeans, so she selected her nicest pair of khaki shorts and a dark teal shirt. She contemplated switching out her favorite flip-flops for sandals but quickly dismissed that idea as she slipped her feet into them. With two minutes to spare, she pocketed her phone and grabbed her room key, then hurried out the door. She swung by the office, but Emma had already left for the day. Rounding the corner by the pool, she stopped in her tracks. Peyton, dressed in white shorts and a blue blouse, stood waiting, an inviting smile on her face. Even though Logan had been exposed to Peyton in nothing but a bikini—and a sleep shirt when they watched the moon—she looked absolutely striking in her summer clothes. Logan blinked several times, noting how the color of Peyton's blouse brought out the blueness of her eyes. She spoke the words that were tumbling around in her mind.

"You're beautiful."

Peyton's smile never faltered. "Thank you. I'd hoped this wasn't too casual."

"No, no. Perfect."

Logan led them back to the boardwalk and to the beach. The Conch was only a few hundred yards down, an easy walk. She took her flip-flops off as soon as they reached the sand, and Peyton followed suit, removing her sandals as well.

"I had fun playing today," Peyton said. "Thank you."

"Me too. In fact, you wore me out. I had to take a nap this afternoon," she said.

Peyton laughed quietly. "Yes, so did I."

Logan grinned mischievously. "Good. Then we should both be well rested. We might have to make it a long night."

"Oh?"

"You know. A view of one day past the full midnight moon."

Peyton laughed again. "Do you plan on banging on my door in the middle of the night again?"

"Well, I may not have to." Logan smiled at her. "This is a date, you know."

"A date?" Peyton shook her head. "Um…no. I don't recall agreeing to a date."

"Sure you did. I said, 'How about an early dinner?' and you said 'I'd love to.' Then I said, 'Great, it's a date.' Or something like that," she added quickly.

"I'm fairly certain that's not how it went," Peyton said.

"No? Well, that's how I remember it," she said. She bumped her shoulder lightly as they walked on. "Too late now anyway. It's already a date."

Peyton said nothing, but Logan noted a smile was still on her face. So okay, it *could* be a date.

Conversation ceased as they walked on, with only an occasional comment about a diving tern and a small flock of white pelicans as they circled overhead, their huge wings spread out to catch the waning sunlight. There would be no view of a sunset from here, though. The backside of the island prevented any views of the bay and the reflection of the sun.

"Here we go," Logan said when the Conch came into view. "Now remember, we're sneaking in," she said with a teasing hint of conspiracy in her voice.

"I can't believe I'm doing this," Peyton said. "Are you sure we won't get in trouble?"

"Only if we get caught," she said with a quick laugh.

She linked fingers with Peyton and casually led her over beyond the dunes as if they had every right to be there. Tables had been set up on the sand and strings of colorful lights hung from the palm trees. Jimmy Buffett was singing about a blonde stranger and a margarita machine was spinning its frozen goodness.

"Oh, yeah," Logan murmured. "My kind of party."

The buffet table was just being set up as waiters brought out various dishes of seafood. Logan spied the shrimp and her mouth watered.

"Did you see that huge platter of fried shrimp?" Logan rubbed her hands together in anticipation, causing Peyton to laugh at her.

"That's your weakness?"

"That...and, well, obviously you in a bikini," she said with a wink. She was pleased by the slight blush that lit Peyton's face. "I'm going to see if I can steal a margarita. You want one?"

"Sure."

Before she could turn, she saw her friend Matt heading their way. She leaned closer to Peyton. "Looks like we're busted," she whispered.

Matt walked purposefully toward them, and Peyton stepped closer to Logan as if for protection. He was tall and lanky, dressed this evening in baggy white slacks and a turquoise shirt. He had an appropriate scowl on his face.

"Crashing the party again?"

Logan shrugged. "I smelled the shrimp a mile away."

"I thought it was the slush of the margarita machine that drew you."

"That too."

Matt finally grinned and pulled her into a quick hug. "Glad you came."

She laughed. "Thank you."

Peyton eyed her suspiciously. "So crashing a party, huh?"

Logan grinned. "Well, I kinda had an invitation." She pointed at Matt. "This is Matthew Canton, an old, dear friend. Matt, meet my new friend, Peyton...something."

Matt didn't bother with a handshake. He hugged her as if they were old friends as well.

"Nice to meet you, Peyton...something." He glanced at Logan with a raised eyebrow.

"We haven't actually exchanged last names," Logan explained.

"Oh. An anonymous holiday romance." He smiled. "I *like* it."

Peyton shook her head. "No, no. Not a romance."

"Not yet," Logan countered. She looked at Matt. "She thinks I'm a stalker."

"Aren't you?" Peyton asked, her mouth hinting at a smile.

"I just liked your bikini."

Matt laughed and shook his finger at her. "Peyton is very lovely. I imagine you were fawning over her." He stood between them and linked arms with them both. "Now, let's find you a drink. And you must try the gumbo. I've outdone myself," he said.

"Are you a chef?" Peyton asked.

"He *thinks* he's a chef," Logan said.

"Careful, my friend, or I will ban you from the shrimp table," Matt warned. He turned to Peyton. "Not a chef, no. I manage the hotel. But I make an excellent gumbo," he said. "Since I'm the boss, they can't throw me out of the kitchen."

"Peyton's ex is a chef," Logan supplied.

"Really? You know that, but you don't know her last name?" He took two plastic glasses and filled each from the margarita machine before handing them over. "Perhaps you need to work on your bedside manner," he said.

Logan grinned at Peyton. "Yeah, I'm hoping she gets a chance to see my bedside manner later," she teased.

"Thank you," Peyton said as she took a swallow of the drink. "It's very good."

"My pleasure. Now, you two enjoy the seafood," he said. "I must mingle. I'll find you at your table later." He turned to go, then stopped. "What about Emma? I met the new woman in her life. Natalie. She's very nice. They said they would try to come by."

"Yes, she said they would," Logan said.

"Great. Then we'll all celebrate your birthday together," he said, then disappeared into a throng of guests.

Logan led them away from the margarita machine after topping off both of their glasses. She had one eye on the shrimp platter across the room as she found an empty table.

"Who's Emma?" Peyton asked.

"My sister. Stepsister, really," she clarified. She pulled out a chair for Peyton before sitting down herself. "I was five when my mother remarried. Emma is a year older than me. She and Matt were in the same grade in school."

Peyton nodded. "And is it a coincidence that the manager of Rainbow Island Resort is also named Emma?"

Logan stopped in mid-drink, her mind scrambling for an explanation. None came. But the look in Peyton's eyes was amusement, not annoyance. She put her drink down, a sheepish smile on her face.

"Well, they might be the same person," she said carefully. "In fact, they kinda are."

"Which is how you got my room number?"

"I had to beat it out of her," Logan said quickly. "I mean, there *are* privacy rules, you know."

Peyton laughed. "And do you do that often? Get her to give you room numbers?"

"No. Really. This was the very first time." Logan leaned closer. "I'm telling you, it's the bikini. And I so want to take it off of you," she said, her voice low, hoping she hadn't overstepped her boundary.

With elbows on the table, Peyton rested her chin on her hands, her gaze traveling across Logan's face. Logan met her stare, the blueness of her eyes dimmed somewhat by the muted lighting. But there wasn't even a hint of anger in those eyes. It was something else entirely, she noted.

"You're not my type at all, you know," Peyton said quietly.

"So you've said." She smiled slightly. "But you find me charming and irresistible, right?"

Peyton smiled too. "Something like that, yes."

"Great. So if I left and brought back a massive plate of shrimp, would that help my case or not?"

"I'm going to say that will definitely help your case," Peyton said. "I love shrimp too."

"My kinda gal," Logan said as she stood. "They've got all kinds of stuff, not just shrimp. Clams, crab, fried fish. And of course, gumbo."

"I'm not crazy about clams, but I do like fish," Peyton said. "I can help," she offered.

"No, that's okay. You save the table. I'll be right back."

Logan hurried off, a satisfied smile on her face. So Peyton thought she was charming and irresistible. Yes, the night was definitely looking up.

CHAPTER ELEVEN

Peyton sipped from her drink, her eyes following Logan as she headed to the buffet table. It was out of character for her, sure, but she truly did find Logan charming. And perhaps a little irresistible as well. To say she was captivated by her would not be an understatement.

What am I doing?

She was living dangerously, that's what. At least for her. The look in Logan's eyes told her exactly how she wanted the night to end. Peyton wasn't *that* out of touch that she couldn't see it. A holiday romance? Dare she? It had been a fun few days. Logan made it fun. She was carefree and easygoing, a smile always on her face. She was entertaining. She was spontaneous. And she was attractive and sexy, and she flirted with a confident ease that left Peyton incapable of resisting.

Because it had simply been too long. Too long without another's touch. Too long without intimacy. Logan was offering to put an end to all that, and Peyton decided she was willing to let her. The fact that she barely knew the woman was a little disturbing. But only a little.

She watched as Logan—dodging a man carrying three margaritas—returned to the table with two plates loaded with an assortment of seafood, mostly fried. Logan sat them down but motioned back to the buffet.

"Gotta get some of Matt's gumbo," she said. "You want a bowl too?"

"Yes, please."

Logan grabbed a shrimp and popped it in her mouth. "Go ahead and start," she mumbled around the shrimp as she headed off again.

Peyton shook her head but smiled. No, Logan was certainly not like other women she'd dated. Logan didn't put on airs, didn't pretend to be something she wasn't. It was refreshing, actually. So with that, she grabbed her own shrimp, forgoing the plastic forks Logan had tossed on the table, using her fingers instead. And it was every bit as good as it looked.

Logan returned again, this time with two steaming bowls of rice smothered in thick gumbo.

"I saw my sister walk in," Logan said. "I hope you don't mind company."

"That's fine."

Logan leaned closer, her tone conspiratorial. "Listen, don't bring up the room number thing. Emma thinks I'm a stalker too."

If not for the smile playing around her mouth, Peyton would have thought Logan was being serious.

"I'll try to get you off the hook then," she said as she sampled the gumbo. "Oh my God, this is good."

"Nice and spicy," Logan said around a mouthful, then smiled as two women approached.

Peyton recognized Emma from the hotel and smiled up at her. "Please join us," she said.

"Emma. Don't know if you remember me," Emma said, holding out her hand in greeting.

"Yes, I do," Peyton said.

"This is my friend, Natalie," Emma said, motioning to the tall woman beside her. "Natalie, this is Peyton. She's staying at our hotel."

"Hi, Natalie," Peyton said. "Nice to meet you," she said politely.

They both pulled out chairs and sat down. "So you're the one Logan's been going on and on about," Natalie said.

Peyton glanced at Logan, who sported an appropriate blush.

"I haven't been going on and on about her," Logan said. "I was simply explaining the color of her bikini."

Natalie and Emma laughed. "How difficult is it to describe red?"

Peyton found Logan absolutely adorable at that moment as their eyes met. Peyton was at a loss for words and her gaze dropped to Logan's lips. A slow smile formed on those lips and Peyton returned it.

"So how's Matt's famous gumbo?" Emma asked, breaking the spell.

"Very good," Peyton said.

"Yeah. One of his better ones," Logan said. "You want me to get a bowl for you?"

"Why don't you take Natalie," Emma suggested. "I'd love a margarita too."

Logan stood, then pointed her finger at Emma. "No telling tales," she warned.

"I'm sure we have more interesting things to talk about than you," Emma said. As soon as they were gone, Emma leaned closer. "Logan can be a handful," she said. "I hope she's not been pestering you to death."

Peyton shook her head. "She's delightful, really. And far too charming to be considered a pest."

Emma reached over and squeezed her arm. "I guess you know by now how she got your room number. It was very unprofessional of me, but Logan has a way of—"

Peyton stopped her apology. "No worries. If it had been a problem, I would have come to you immediately."

"Well, regardless of your impression of her, she's harmless. I promise."

Peyton nodded. "I enjoy her company."

Before Emma could say more, Logan returned with two more bowls of gumbo. Natalie followed holding two margaritas, one of which she handed to Emma.

"The seafood buffet looks great," Natalie said. "We'll have to get some later."

"Take some of ours," Peyton offered.

Logan snatched a shrimp quickly. "Yeah, take some of ours," she said as she bit into it.

"You and your shrimp," Emma said with a shake of her head. She looked at Peyton. "This woman eats her weight in shrimp whenever she's down here."

Peyton glanced at Logan. "And how often is that?"

Logan shrugged. "I come to visit three or four times a year, I guess." Then she grinned. "And you're the very first person I've had dinner with." Logan looked at Emma. "Tell her. She thinks I'm a stalker."

Emma laughed. "I have forbidden her from talking to the guests at the hotel. For some reason, she totally ignored my rules when she saw you."

It was Peyton's turn to blush. She met Logan's gaze, knowing exactly what she was thinking. *It was the bikini.* And for some reason, she was very, very thankful she'd purchased the new red bikini before this trip.

Their conversation drifted to many topics, and she enjoyed the sisterly interaction between Emma and Logan. When Matt joined them, the three of them chatted like the old friends they were, regaling her and Natalie with stories of high school and beyond.

"So we sneaked into the pool after hours. This one," Matt said, pointing at Logan, "thought she could do a triple somersault off the high dive."

Emma laughed. "Can you say 'belly buster'?"

Logan held her thumb and forefinger together. "I was this close to nailing it."

"Yeah. And you were this close," Matt said, mimicking her fingers, "to getting us suspended." He turned to Peyton. "We weren't exactly wearing swimsuits."

Peyton laughed. "Why doesn't this surprise me?"

He laughed too. "I've never heard so much hollering and screaming."

"I was not screaming," Logan insisted.

"Oh, yes, you were," Emma said. "You had a bruise on your stomach for a week."

"Okay. So maybe I screamed a little," Logan said, glancing at Peyton. "They're only telling you part of it. Matt bet me ten bucks I wouldn't do it."

"And you never passed up a challenge," he said. "The cleaning crew heard her screaming and came running. Imagine their surprise to find three naked students in the pool."

"Why didn't you get suspended?" Natalie asked.

Matt laughed. "These two naked beauties turned on the charm. The girls promised they wouldn't tell that the doors had been left unlocked if they didn't tell we'd been in there swimming."

"The doors were unlocked?"

"Oh, no. Logan learned to pick locks in the eighth grade," he said.

"Yes, one of the many useful things my father taught me," Logan said with a grin.

The next hour passed quickly. Matt replaced their margarita cups with wineglasses and brought a bottle to the table. They all raised their glasses in a toast to Logan on her birthday.

"Our little girl finally turns thirty," Matt said. "May this birthday be one you'll always remember."

"And may you have many more," Emma added.

"Thank you. I love you guys," Logan said. "And a toast to Peyton as well. Her birthday is coming up in a few weeks."

Logan touched glasses with them all, pausing to wink slightly when she met her eyes. Peyton returned it with a quick smile. In the few seconds their eyes held, she wondered if it would indeed be a night Logan forever remembered. For that matter, would it be one *she* always remembered?

After the wine, Emma and Natalie stood to leave. The sisters hugged tightly and Peyton watched with envy. Her only sister was six years older than she was and they'd never had a close relationship. She couldn't imagine having a bond like Logan and Emma obviously shared.

"Nice to meet you," Natalie told her. "Hope to see you again."

"You too," she said. "Thank you."

Emma leaned close to her. "You can threaten to call me if Logan gets out of hand," she said with a smile.

"I think I can handle her," Peyton said.

Emma nodded. "Yes, I think you can. Have fun, you two," she said with wave as she left.

Matt bent down and kissed Logan's cheek, then walked over and did the same to her. "Great to meet you, Peyton. Thanks for coming by."

"Thanks for letting us crash your party. The gumbo was excellent."

He bowed slightly. "Thank you. Good night, my friends."

Peyton smiled at Logan. "They're really nice. I had a good time."

"Great. So did I."

Peyton folded her hands together and rested her chin there, still looking at Logan. "Good birthday?"

"So far." Logan wiggled her eyebrows. "I can think of a few things that would make it even better."

Peyton wondered what had gotten into her as she leaned closer, her gaze dropping to Logan's mouth. "Only a few?"

"Do you want me to list them all? Should I start with a kiss? Seeing you naked?"

Peyton swallowed, hoping she wasn't in over her head here. She tried to remind herself that she didn't really know this woman. Not really. Not enough to contemplate spending the night with her. But she thought she was a good enough judge of character to know that Logan was indeed harmless. She had just spent the better part of two hours with her and her friends and no alarm bells had gone off. She frowned slightly as she pulled her gaze away. She had also thought she was a good judge of character when she started her relationship with Vicky. But how could she even compare this? Logan would be nothing more than a holiday fling.

She looked back at Logan, seeing eyes that were trusting and honest, open and friendly. She stared into them, knowing she had nothing to fear from her. So she gave in to the desire that Logan had been stoking for the last few days.

"You…you want to head back?" she asked, her voice hinting at the nervousness she felt.

Logan nodded. "If you're ready."

The statement had a double meaning and she knew it. She met Logan's gaze head on, nodding slightly.

"Yes. I think I'm ready."

CHAPTER TWELVE

Logan waited until they were away from the lights of the party before taking her hand. They were walking close together, and Peyton's fingers clung tightly to her own. She had been captivated by this woman from the moment she laid eyes on her, but she wasn't sure how Peyton really felt until about ten minutes ago. She'd hoped the attraction wasn't one-sided and that she hadn't been too obnoxious in her pursuit. But the few minutes they'd sat at the table alone, she'd finally seen what she'd been hoping for. Those baby blues had turned a shade darker, and Logan had seen desire in them—even though she suspected Peyton was still trying to hide it.

Yes, she wanted to ravish her and she could hardly wait to get her naked, but her instincts told her to go slow with Peyton. Very slow.

So she eased their pace, taking them closer to the water. The moon was a couple of hours past rising but not yet high in the sky. Not the inflated and luminous moon they'd viewed the night before but still plenty bright on the water. She paused, watching the light bounce on the waves. It was a warm, pleasant breeze this evening and she sighed contentedly. She felt Peyton's fingers move against hers, and she turned, finding Peyton's eyes on her.

She shifted, bringing Peyton closer. There was enough light for her to see Peyton's eyes clearly. Mixed with the desire she saw was still a little uncertainty, a little fear. She dropped her gaze to Peyton's mouth.

"I'm going to kiss you," she said quietly. She was surprised to see a quick smile on Peyton's lips.

"Do you always warn women before you kiss them?"

"Only when they look terrified that I'm about to."

Peyton's smile faded. "Maybe I was terrified you wouldn't."

As Logan's gaze dropped to her lips again, she realized this wasn't just some college student she was with. Peyton was a mature, grown woman who was perhaps a little out of her element. And as such, Logan was a little out of hers. Nonetheless, Logan felt an overwhelming need to protect her for some reason.

She brought her hand up, lightly grazing Peyton's cheek, noting the quick intake of breath, the darkening of eyes, the rapid pulse at the base of her neck. She felt a tremor and wasn't sure if it was Peyton or herself. She bent closer, her lips lightly brushing against Peyton's, testing her. There was no gesture of retreat, so she deepened the kiss, her eyes closing as she heard a subtle moan from Peyton. She didn't dare take it any further, not out here on the beach. She pulled away slowly, smiling at Peyton's shift in breathing, at the tightening of fingers against hers.

They didn't say anything as they continued on up the beach, the water lapping near them as high tide approached. When they reached the break in the dunes that would take them to the boardwalk and their hotel, Logan hesitated.

"If you're not sure, not comfortable, we don't—"

"Don't spoil the mood, Logan," Peyton said.

Logan smiled. "No. I wouldn't dare. Come on."

Again, no words were spoken and the only sound was their footsteps on the boardwalk. They heard laughter coming from the clothing optional pool and Logan glanced over, seeing four woman playing in the water.

"Don't even think about it," Peyton said as she tugged Logan away.

Logan laughed quietly, then motioned around the corner. "My room's on the first floor."

She fumbled with her key, finally getting the door opened. She left the light off as she closed the door behind them. They stood facing each other in the darkness.

"I…I don't normally do things like this," Peyton said. "In fact—"

"Shhh," Logan stopped her with a gentle finger on her lips. "It's just us. No one else."

Peyton then surprised her by parting her lips, her tongue coming out to brush against the finger that still rested there. It was enough to provoke Logan into action, pulling Peyton flush against her body before finding her mouth with her own. Her intentions to go slow were jettisoned the instant Peyton's body molded itself to hers. Quiet moans mingled as hands moved at will, pulling each other closer still.

Logan actually felt her knees go weak when their kiss deepened, their tongues dueling for control. When she felt Peyton's hands slip under her shirt she knew she'd underestimated her. She smiled against her lips, getting one in return.

"Can we take this off?" Peyton whispered, her fingers already working on the buttons of her shirt.

"Absolutely."

Logan's shirt fell to the floor, but she stopped Peyton when she would have unhooked her bra. Instead, she made fast work of Peyton's blouse, letting it drop where her own had landed. Logan's heart was beating quickly in anticipation. There was just enough light in the room for her to make out Peyton's features, and she watched the rapid rise and fall of Peyton's chest, evidence of her own arousal.

Logan reached out, her fingers running gently around the edge of Peyton's bra, seeing Peyton's breath catch as she touched the soft swell that was barely hidden by the lacy material. She continued her movements, feeling Peyton's nipple harden as she brushed against it.

She lowered her head, her mouth moving across Peyton's neck, then lower, following the path her fingers had taken seconds earlier. Peyton's breath was coming faster and the hands resting lightly at Logan's waist tightened as her tongue flicked out, touching her nipple through the thin material of her bra.

The moan Peyton let slip out was Logan's undoing. She reached behind her, fumbling only slightly with the hook before releasing the clasp. Peyton stepped away, letting Logan remove her bra. Logan's mouth watered as she stared at her, her breasts full and firm, her nipples rock hard.

"Beautiful," she whispered as her hands cupped her, her thumbs raking across each nipple, causing Peyton to draw in a quick breath.

"Yours," Peyton said. "Off."

Logan did as she asked, nearly ripping the bra from her body in her haste to get naked. Peyton drew her down to the bed and Logan followed, resting her weight on top. Peyton guided her to her breasts and Logan's mouth covered her, her tongue swirling around a taut nipple before drawing it inside, sucking gently. Peyton moaned again, her hips moving instinctively against Logan. Logan pressed down, groaning in frustration as their shorts prevented the contact she craved. She released Peyton's nipple long enough to unbutton her shorts, then Peyton's. Impatient hands shoved them down and they kicked them off, finally, at last, leaving them naked.

Peyton's thighs parted and Logan slipped between them, her mouth returning to Peyton's breast, then back to her mouth, their tongues again brushing wetly against the other. Peyton cupped Logan's hips, pulling her hard against her as her thighs parted even further.

"God, I can feel how wet you are," Logan murmured against her mouth as she thrust against her.

"Yes," Peyton breathed. "It's been…it's been a long time since…I've been with someone."

Logan kissed her hard. "Then I'm going to make you come all night long," she said, finding her nipple again, her lips closing around it.

She shifted slightly, her hand moving between them, feeling their wetness as it coated their thighs. With her fingers, she opened Peyton, exposing her clit. She thrust forward, opening herself as well until their clits were touching. Peyton moaned loudly as Logan moved against her, grinding their centers together.

"Dear *God*," Peyton groaned, her hands holding Logan firmly to her.

Logan was shocked to feel her orgasm building already and she hoped Peyton was close too. It was too exhilarating to even think about slowing down. She thrust harder against her, gasping for breath as their clits slammed together.

"Oh...*yes*," Peyton hissed as her hips jerked hard against Logan. Her body buckled as she climaxed and Logan gave in to her own orgasm, feeling herself pulsing against Peyton as she continued to keep them pressed together.

"*Jesus*," she breathed as she collapsed on top of Peyton. "I didn't mean for it to be so quick," she said, her breathing still ragged.

"There's nothing wrong with fast," Peyton said, her hands still moving lightly against Logan's bare back.

"No?"

Peyton surprised her by rolling them over, Peyton now on top. "But slow is good too," she said.

Logan sucked in her breath as Peyton's mouth found its way to her breast. "Yeah, slow is good too," she murmured, her eyes closing as Peyton's lips closed over her nipple. "Very good."

CHAPTER THIRTEEN

Peyton stretched her legs out, her sore muscles protesting after their night of activity. She felt Logan's warm body next to her and she opened her eyes, wondering what time it was. The room was still dark so she closed them again as she felt Logan stir. Logan rolled toward her, then slipped an arm across her waist possessively. Peyton turned, letting her lips brush against Logan's face.

She should be exhausted. She *was* exhausted. But after nearly a year of neglect, her body was still making demands. Even though they'd been in bed for hours and Logan had made good on her promise—Peyton had indeed come all night long—her body still wanted more.

Logan's eyes opened and she smiled as Peyton's hand moved over her hip and along the curve of her waist.

Peyton smiled too. "It's like someone has taken over my body," she tried to explain.

"Yeah. It was me," Logan said. Then she sat up. "Come on."

"Come on, what?"

"Bathroom break, then we have to go."

"Go? Go where?"

Logan stood beside the bed, naked. She tilted her head to Peyton. "It's almost dawn," she said as if that explained it.

Peyton closed her eyes, not moving. And Logan was back to being Logan, she thought with a smile. "And that means what?"

Logan pulled the covers off her. "That means…skinny-dipping."

Peyton sat up, trying to reach for the covers. "Oh, no. No, no, no. I will *not* go skinny-dipping."

"Come on, Peyton. It'll be fun."

And that, of course, was all it took. She swung her legs out of bed, telling herself to no avail that she did not—ever—go skinny-dipping. Apparently that was about to change.

They put on the same clothes they'd worn the night before, neither of them bothering with underwear or bras. Peyton was shocked at the time. It was nearly five, but the sky wasn't yet showing the first signs of dawn. Darkness still hovered over the beach.

Logan took her hand and led her to the private pool. The few lights in the water were a mix of red and yellow, making the pool sensuously inviting. Nonetheless, she was still nervous.

As if sensing that, Logan pulled her closer. "We're all alone."

The brush of her body dispelled some of her nervousness and Peyton savored the gentle kiss that Logan gave her. Her pulse sprang to life at the contact, making her very aware that neither of them was wearing anything beneath their clothes. Logan deepened the kiss, her tongue tracing Peyton's lower lip before slipping inside. Peyton's mouth opened, moaning into the kiss as Logan slipped a thigh between her legs.

"Have you ever made love in the water?" Logan whispered.

Had she? She had her own pool. She and Vicky had shared it, surely. But at that moment, she was having a hard time recalling Vicky's face, much less if they'd ever made love in her pool.

"No. Am I about to?"

Logan's answer was a sexy grin, and she stripped off her clothes. Peyton stood frozen in place as Logan walked to the edge of the pool and dove in with barely a ripple.

God, she's got a great body.

And Peyton wanted it. Again.

She quickly took off her own clothing, tossing it on the lounge chair where they'd tossed their towels earlier. Logan was waiting for her, and she dove in too, although not quite as gracefully as Logan had. The water was cool but not overly so. She swam over to Logan. She had to admit, it was indeed freeing to be in the water totally naked. It had a completely different feel than when wearing a suit.

"Nice," she said. "It feels…sensuous."

"Yes. There's nothing like it."

Logan led them to shallower water; it was just above their waists. She felt the hard edge of the pool against her back as Logan came closer, her hands sliding over and around her body, the water making her feel weightless as Logan lifted her, bringing her to rest on her thigh.

Their kiss was heated, wet, their mouths clashing as their tongues battled. There was no preamble as Logan entered her, and Peyton didn't need there to be. She was ready and she moaned as Logan's fingers filled her. Their mouths were still joined, their kisses changing between tongues and lips and back to tongues. Logan had one arm around her waist, holding her up as her other hand moved between them, her fingers slipping in and out of her quickly, her thumb raking across her clit with each stroke.

"Can you feel it?" Logan whispered, her mouth moving to Peyton's ear. "I wish that was my tongue instead of my fingers."

Peyton moaned as she pictured just that.

"I would suck your clit into my mouth, make you scream my name."

The words rang in her ear as she recalled Logan doing that very thing during the night. She was panting as she clung to Logan, the water splashing between them as Logan's fingers still plunged inside of her.

"When we get back to the room, I'm going to devour you with my mouth," Logan said, her lips still moving against her ear. "My tongue inside of you, not my fingers. You'll be so wet and I'll drink it all, I'll eat every bit of you, I'll—"

But Peyton heard no more as the roar of her orgasm rendered her deaf. She tried to muffle her scream against Logan's shoulder as she felt her world spin. She squeezed her thighs together, holding Logan's fingers deep inside of her.

"Dear God," she gasped. "That was…unbelievable."

With her arms draped across Logan's shoulders, she straddled Logan's waist, wrapping her legs around her as they bobbed gently in the water. Logan's mouth found her nipple and Peyton threw her head back, relishing the feeling as Logan's tongue flicked against it. It was only then that Logan withdrew her fingers and Peyton was shocked to realize she was still so incredibly aroused. She didn't know if it was the water or Logan's earlier words or simply Logan herself, but Peyton wanted to devour *her*…right then, right there.

Feeling daring, feeling as if someone had indeed taken over her body, she dropped her legs from around Logan and stood, her gaze fiery hot as she stared at her.

"I want you. Now."

She didn't wait for a reply. She led Logan into the shallow end and up on the steps.

"Sit. Lie back."

Logan did her bidding, and Peyton knelt down on the bottom step. She spread Logan's thighs, revealing her glistening wetness. Peyton felt nearly delirious as she buried her face there, moaning as she tasted Logan. Her tongue rubbed against her clit, then lower, slipping inside her. Logan's hips jerked and Peyton held them down. She moved back to her clit, sucking it hard inside her mouth, loving the sounds coming from Logan as she feasted on her. She heard Logan panting, felt Logan's hand in her hair, recognized the arch of her hips as she neared orgasm but she didn't want it to end. She hadn't had her fill yet, but Logan climaxed anyway, jerking up hard as she screamed out, then holding Peyton's mouth to her, her tongue pressed hard against her clit, feeling it pulse against it.

"God, woman," Logan murmured as her hand relaxed.

Peyton still couldn't pull her mouth away. She moved her lips back and forth, still tasting her, causing Logan to jerk with each touch. She ran her tongue up and down the length of her, taking care to avoid her sensitive clit. She could have stayed there for hours, but Logan finally pulled her up.

They slipped back into the water, embracing tightly, their bodies pressed together. Their kisses were gentle, lips moving slowly against lips, kisses that made Peyton's heart flutter with each pass. They floated like that for long minutes, kissing, touching, caressing. They only parted when they became aware of dawn approaching. The sky was turning a soft pink and the first calls of morning were heard as gulls raced to the shore.

They got out of the pool together, and Logan tossed her a towel.

"So how was your first skinny-dipping experience?"

Peyton laughed quietly. "Quite enjoyable. Thank you."

Logan grinned. "No. Thank *you*. That was the best birthday ever."

Peyton sighed. "Good. But I'm totally exhausted."

"Yeah? I thought you had great stamina for your age."

Peyton slipped her shirt on. "Not a great morning-after line," she said. "Try again."

Logan laughed. "I'm teasing. I'm thirty now, you know. We're practically the same age."

"I'll be thirty-five in less than a month. That's *not* practically the same age." And reminding herself of her age and her lack of sleep, she had to cover a yawn. "I'm so tired."

"My bed is available," Logan offered.

Peyton shook her head. "I'm afraid we would get little sleep," she said as she watched Logan slip her shorts on. Her hands itched to take them off again.

"So I shouldn't offer coffee and breakfast?"

"Maybe later," she said. She walked closer, kissing Logan lightly on the lips. "I had a wonderful time. Thank you."

Logan nodded. "I'll see you again, right?"

She frowned. "I don't even know what day it is."

"Thursday," Logan supplied. "Did you lose some days?"

She laughed. "It feels like it. I'm going to get some sleep. Find me later," she said, having no doubt that Logan would.

She felt Logan watching her as she walked away, but she dared not turn around. If Logan had prompted only slightly, she would have gone back to her room with her. But she suspected Logan was as tired as she was.

It was only as she was opening the door to her own room that she let the magnitude of the evening—the night, the morning—hit her. She'd just had the most incredible sex of her life with a woman she had only known for a few days. She paused, expecting to feel shame or even regret. She was surprised she felt neither.

Instead, she slipped out of her clothes and fell into bed. After being dormant for so long, her body was very much alive. She smiled contentedly, wondering what the next couple of days would bring.

CHAPTER FOURTEEN

Logan stretched her arms over her head and let out a loud yawn before plopping herself down in one of Emma's chairs. She'd managed to sleep until nearly noon, finding herself in the same position when she woke up as when she'd crashed. Even though she was still tired, she couldn't keep the smile off her face. The night—and morning—had been fantastic.

Emma hung up the phone, finally giving Logan her full attention. A slow smile formed on her face.

"Well, don't you look all…glowing," Emma said.

"Glowing? Don't know if I'd use that word. Extremely—*extremely*—sated, if anything," she said with a grin. "It was the best birthday ever. If they were all like last night, I might actually start to celebrate them."

"I'm happy for you." Then she paused. "Peyton's not going to, like, press charges or anything, right?"

Logan laughed. "I wouldn't think so. Especially since our time together didn't end until dawn. Down in the pool," she added with a wink.

"God, you did it in the pool? You've always been obsessed with skinny-dipping. It's a wonder you haven't been arrested," Emma said with a laugh.

"Yeah, yeah," Logan said dismissively. "Now, where's she from?"

"Peyton?" Emma shook her head. "No. Absolutely not."

"Come on, Emma," Logan pleaded.

"No. It's one thing for you to stalk her here. But I will not give you her address so you can stalk her at her home."

"I'm not going to stalk her," Logan promised. "I just want to know where she lives."

Emma shook her head. "If she wants you to know, she'll tell you."

Logan blew out her breath. "I guess." Then, "Will you at least give me her last name?"

Emma laughed. "No. Ask her yourself if you want to know."

Logan knew by the look on Emma's face that she wasn't going to divulge Peyton's personal information. Giving up her room number was one thing. Her home address quite another. Well, she supposed Emma was right. If Peyton wanted her to know, she'd tell her.

"Okay. Then how about lunch? I was going to drive over to the Taco Barn. You want some?"

"Sounds great," she said as her phone rang. "Get me three. Mix and match," she said before answering.

Logan nodded and left Emma to her work. She paused outside, then headed around to the pool. A quick glance around told her Peyton was not up yet. Still in bed, under the covers, most likely. That thought made her smile, knowing she was the reason for Peyton's exhaustion.

Yeah, it had been a great birthday.

*　*　*

On her way to the shower, Peyton was startled by the ringing of her phone. She stared at it for the longest time, only then realizing she hadn't even looked at the thing in nearly three days.

She sprang into action, snatching it up as she recognized Susan's ringtone.

"What's wrong?"

Susan laughed. "Why do you assume something's wrong?"

"Because you said you wouldn't call me unless there was an emergency," she reminded her.

"That was because I assumed you would check in a couple of times every day. Since I hadn't heard from you…"

Peyton smiled. "I took your advice. I've been relaxing. Recharging," she said.

"That's great. So you're having fun?"

At that, Peyton blushed freely. "Yes. I've been having…fun."

"So we don't need to worry about you?"

"No. Actually, I've met a few people here. I had dinner with a group of them last night, in fact." And that was technically the truth, she told herself. She saw no reason to go into the whys and hows of the group dinner, no reason to mention Logan's name.

"Well, good for you," Susan said. "I was afraid you'd spend the whole time in your room reading. Did you at least get out on the beach?"

"Yes. I've been to the beach. And I have done some reading, but it was by the pool. So I'm having a nice, relaxing time. Thank you for making me do this," she said.

"You're welcome. And I'll let you get back to it, then. Your flight is on Saturday? Are you sure you don't need me to pick you up?"

"No. I left my car there, but thank you."

"Okay. Then I guess I'll see you on Monday in the office. Can't wait to hear all about your trip."

"See you then."

She tossed her phone down, wondering how much she would tell Susan. She shrugged. She could tell her nothing, or she could tell her everything. She could imagine Susan's shocked face should she tell her about last night. To say it was out of character for her would be an understatement.

Oh, well. She wasn't going to worry about it. Right now, all she wanted was a shower and something to eat. And then she wanted to slip into her bikini and head to the pool.

Later, she hoped, Logan would slip that bikini off of her. *God.*

She met her reflection in the mirror, wondering who that woman was that was smiling back at her.

CHAPTER FIFTEEN

Logan smiled broadly when she spotted Peyton heading to the chaise lounge by the pool. She glanced at her half-eaten burrito, wondering how quickly she could finish it.

"I take it by the look on your face that Peyton is out there?" Emma asked with a quick glance out her window.

Logan wiped the smile away. "I'm sure I don't have a *look*," she said as she bit into her burrito.

"You seem quite taken with her, sis. I don't know that you've ever been out with anyone older than twenty-five, much less slept with them."

"I'm not taken with her," Logan said with a shake of her head. "She's cute and sexy and we had a good time together." She put her burrito down, considering Emma's comment. "You're right. I don't think I've ever been out with anyone older than twenty-five. In fact, twenty-four might be more accurate." She sipped from her tea. "Why do you think that is?"

Emma shrugged. "Not sure. Maybe you just got into the habit of dating college girls."

"Well, yeah. I was in college once. I'm thirty, though. What's my excuse now?"

Emma finished off her last taco, then wiped her mouth. "Please don't get offended," she started. "But I think a lot of it is because of your father."

"Ted? Why?"

"He's very laid-back. He doesn't get too worked up about anything. He likes to have fun. He'd rather go fishing than go to work."

"Who wouldn't?"

"Yes, but most people *still* go to work even if they'd rather be fishing. Not your dad."

"Okay. So he's not exactly responsible. I hope you're not implying that I'm not either," she said.

"Of course not. I know that without you the painting business would have folded years ago. But you like to have fun too. And that's great. Everyone should. But as we get older, we have more responsibilities and less time to do things on a whim. Yet you also have your dad's laid-back streak. And you're as spontaneous today as you were in high school," Emma said.

"Okay. So what are you trying to say?"

"I'm saying, you still have that side of you where you want to blow off work and head to the lake. But most people can't do that. Unless you don't work or you're a college student and you can blow off class."

Logan smiled but shook her head. "That's your reasoning as to why I date college students? Because they don't have adult responsibilities yet?" Logan leaned forward. "You don't think it has to do with long legs, tan bodies and how they look in a bikini?"

Emma leaned forward too. "Then why are you salivating over a thirty-five-year-old woman out there?"

"I'm not salivating," she said. "Much. But you've seen her in her bikini."

"Exactly. And she's not a college student. And you are too salivating over her."

Logan laughed. "Well, if you'd had the night—and morning—that I had, you'd be salivating too."

Emma smiled. "I have my own to salivate over, thank you very much."

Logan folded up the rest of her burrito and tossed it in the trash. "I like Natalie. She's good for you."

"Meaning she doesn't come with baggage."

"You said it, not me."

Emma nodded. "It's refreshing, really. There's no drama with her. When's the last time I was able to say that about someone I was dating?"

"Never."

Emma folded up her trash too, then waved Logan away. "Go already."

Logan grinned. "Thanks, sis."

"Thanks for lunch. Enjoy your afternoon."

"I hope to."

"Don't get into trouble," Emma added just as Logan closed the door.

Logan found she was actually whistling as she headed to the pool. She stopped, trying to compose herself. Geez, you'd think she'd never been with a woman before. So she took a deep breath before going through the gate, her gaze traveling across the handful of other women out there before landing on Peyton.

She was stretched out on the lounge, her blonde hair brushed back from her face, sunglasses covering those baby blues. Logan took all that in quickly even though her eyes were glued to the tiny bikini top covering her breasts. A black bikini today, she noted as her gaze traveled across her stomach, hips and legs, then back up.

Yes, she was indeed salivating. She swallowed, then walked closer. Peyton turned her head although Logan couldn't see her eyes for the sunglasses.

Logan raised her eyebrows. "Your skin is glistening. I see you took my advice and used lotion today."

Peyton slowly shoved her sunglasses up, revealing the eyes that Logan wanted to fall into. Peyton smiled and Logan did the same.

"Yes, I did."

Logan tilted her head, her gaze again making a trek across Peyton's body. "I didn't think it could get any better than the red bikini," she said. "But...wow," she whispered.

"And why do you have so many clothes on?"

"If you want to take them off of me, you can."

Peyton laughed. "I'm not sure I've recovered yet."

"No?" Logan pulled a chair closer and sat down, stretching her legs out. "Well, I didn't want to tempt you, so I thought I'd wear shorts."

"Tempt me? I remember exactly what you look like without clothes on," Peyton said quietly.

Logan met her eyes, feeling a flutter in her stomach. "Yeah? So when do you think you will have recovered?"

Peyton raised an eyebrow questioningly.

"Because I want to take that bikini off of you."

Peyton smiled. "I thought you liked it."

"Yes, I love it. And I'm going to love it more as I'm slipping it off your body." She was pleased to see Peyton's eyes darken, pleased to hear her quick intake of breath. "I think I'd really like to do that right now," she continued, her voice not much more than a whisper. "I'm going to take your top off first. Then I'm going to touch your nipples with my tongue, my mouth." She paused. "I'm going to suck on them until you beg me to stop." She swallowed, her own breathing becoming ragged. "Then I'm going to slip your bottom off. You're going to be so wet by that time. Then I'm—"

"Okay...okay." Peyton jumped up and grabbed Logan's hand, pulling her after her. "I've recovered enough."

They raced to Logan's room and she was embarrassed to find her hand shaking as she tried to get the door opened. Damn, but she was aroused and she had yet to touch her. They fell inside, and Logan kicked the door shut with her foot, smiling as Peyton beckoned her to come closer.

"Now, what were you going to do first?"

CHAPTER SIXTEEN

Peyton stared at the sign above the door, then looked back at Logan.

"I don't feel comfortable going in there," she admitted. "I've never—"

"It'll be fun," Logan said.

Peyton tried to push her embarrassment aside. After all, she knew no one in Corpus Christi. The fact that she had never, not once, set foot inside a store selling sex toys was beside the point. After spending over an hour in bed and then sharing a shower, Logan had suggested a trip into Corpus. "Something to play with tonight," she'd said. Of course, Logan's hand had been between her legs at the time and Peyton would have probably agreed to almost anything.

She looked again at the closed door. It appeared dark inside. She imagined a sleazy man, probably overweight with greasy hair, waiting behind a glassed cage. He would leer at them as they entered, probably demanding ID and a secret code to enter into the shadowy niches of the sex toy store.

Dare she? She took a deep breath and nodded at Logan, bravely following her inside the store. But the dark window belied the interior of the store. It was bright and well lit, cheery almost. She smiled at her earlier thoughts. There was no fat, greasy-haired man staring at them. A young woman was behind the counter, and she barely glanced their way, her attention on the iPad she held.

There were a few other people in the store, mostly talking in low tones. Two girls who looked barely college age started giggling as they browsed through rows and rows of dildos.

"So what do you like?" Logan whispered.

Peyton gave her a slow smile. "Don't you know by now?"

Logan leaned closer. "Well, I mean besides my mouth all over your body."

Peyton felt Logan's breath on her ear, and it sent a shiver down her spine. She met Logan's gaze, remembering exactly where that mouth had been only a short hour ago.

"I've never used…toys," she admitted. "I wouldn't know where to begin."

She wasn't certain if she expected a teasing retort from Logan or perhaps a mention of her boring and conservative dating history, but the soft, rather sweet smile she got was not it. Logan's fingers tightened around hers for a quick moment.

"Then we won't get too crazy," Logan said. "Let's just look around. We don't have to get anything if you don't want to."

Peyton returned the squeeze against her fingers. "I trust you."

Logan leaned closer and brushed her lips against Peyton's mouth. "Good."

Peyton looked around quickly, seeing if anyone had seen the kiss. That—a kiss in public—she was not used to. Her embarrassment returned tenfold as she stared, open-mouthed, at a harness and whip.

"No, no, no," Logan said. "I'm not into that. Over here," she said, leading her around the corner. "Vibrators." She motioned farther down. "Dildos."

Peyton's gaze traveled over what appeared to be hundreds of choices, all different colors, sizes and shapes. She was at a loss for words.

"Oh, the Luv Bunny," Logan said, pointing. She grinned at her. "Sounds interesting."

"What in the world do you *do* with all of this stuff?" Peyton asked in a whisper.

"Alas, if I only had the time to show you," Logan said dramatically. She picked up one of the vibrators, scanning the information on it. "Eight-function G-spot vibrator," she said. "'Select your favorite function using the built-in push button at the base,'" she read, "'and enjoy intense pleasure throughout the silky smooth shaft.'" Logan met her eyes and smiled. "'The tip is angled to specifically target the G-spot for amazing climaxes.'"

Peyton swallowed nervously.

"As an added bonus," Logan said, her voice dropping to a whisper. "It's waterproof."

At that, Peyton laughed. "I'm guessing you want to try it in the pool."

Logan's eyes turned serious. "Can we?"

Peyton could do nothing more than nod. This entire vacation had been so out of character for her, beginning with taking it in the first place. But meeting Logan, sleeping with her—having the best sex of her life—and now shopping for sex toys had her head spinning. She was so far out of her element, so far removed from her life as the boring, conservative accountant, that she hardly recognized herself. And now here she stood, in the middle of a sex toy store, contemplating which vibrator to buy so that they could use it in the pool. She couldn't help but wonder what her friends would think of her.

As if sensing her self-doubts, Logan said, "You know, we don't have to get anything. It's not like it hasn't been fantastic as it is."

Peyton stared at her. "Has it been?"

"God, yes. For me anyway. I thought for you too. But if—"

"No. I mean, yes. Yes, it has been," she said quickly. "I'm sorry. All this," she said, waving her hand. "I feel so sheltered," she admitted. "So *old.*"

Logan shook her head. "You're not old, Peyton." She put the vibrator back. "Come on. Let's get an early dinner. I know a place on the bay."

"Okay." Peyton glanced back at the vibrator, then smiled. "Can we still get it?"

* * *

Logan covered Peyton's mouth with her own, trying to stifle her scream as she climaxed. Peyton jerked her mouth away, gasping for breath as her body convulsed.

"Logan...*Jesus*," Peyton whispered as her arms fell limply to her sides. "You're killing me."

"But we haven't tried it in the pool yet," Logan said with a grin, her lips moving lazily to Peyton's breasts. She was surprised Peyton still had the energy to moan as she suckled her nipple.

"You've got to stop," Peyton said. "I won't be able to walk tomorrow."

Logan pulled her mouth away from Peyton's breast. She rolled Peyton to her side, then snuggled up behind her, wrapping her arms around her. Peyton sighed contentedly as she pulled Logan's arms tighter around her.

"Yes. Just let me rest for a minute," Peyton murmured.

Logan smiled against her neck, then untangled their hands long enough to bring the sheet over them. She too needed to rest. After an early dinner in which their conversation had touched on numerous topics, from childhood vacations to siblings, she still didn't know where Peyton lived although she assumed it was somewhere in Texas. She had come close to asking several times, but Emma's words were still fresh. If Peyton wanted her to know, she'd tell her. So a light dinner and a walk along the bay, then back to the resort where they had once again found themselves in Logan's room. Their sex toy was momentarily forgotten as they raced to undress, then hands and mouths were everywhere at once and they fell into bed together. Their first orgasms came quick. It was Peyton who remembered the toy as they'd been lying there recovering.

"Oh, yeah. We bought something to help with that, didn't we?"

And now, two hours later, they were both at the brink of exhaustion. She heard Peyton's even breathing and knew she was already asleep. Logan closed her eyes, enjoying the closeness, the aftermath of their lovemaking. She snuggled a little closer and let sleep claim her too.

CHAPTER SEVENTEEN

Never in her life had she felt so…so sexual. Peyton stretched out, loving the feel of the cool sheets against her naked body. She was still a bit drowsy, but she felt relaxed in a dreamy sort of way. Relaxed and oh, so satisfied. She smiled and rolled over, ignoring the soreness of her muscles. She would guess she'd had more sex in the last few days than she'd had in the last few years combined. That in itself spoke volumes on the state of hers and Vicky's relationship. But she didn't want to think about that now.

No, now she wanted to get as close as possible to the naked woman lying next to her. Logan was still asleep, on her side facing Peyton. If she weren't so tired, she would wake Logan and suggest a skinny-dipping trip before dawn, but that would mean they'd have to get out of bed. Her gaze lingered on Logan, past the lips that were parted slightly and up to her eyelids that fluttered as if she were deep in a dream. Peyton took this opportunity to observe her freely. She knew Logan was only thirty, but in sleep she looked even younger. Her face was smooth and flawless and nicely tanned. She had to stop herself from reaching out and touching it. She already knew how soft her skin was. She'd felt it with her hands and her mouth.

She sighed, knowing their time together was nearing its end. This would be their last day. She would be leaving the next morning and she assumed Logan was as well. She remembered her saying she was staying until Saturday.

She was a bit surprised that Logan hadn't asked her again where she lived, hadn't asked what her last name was. But it didn't matter. They were from two different worlds and this was nothing more than a holiday affair. She would remember it always, of course. How could she not? But when she returned to Austin, it would be back to reality. And the reality was, she was a boring, conservative accountant with boring, conservative friends. She smiled, knowing some of them would be offended by her description, however true it may be.

But she still had one more day. One more day to be carefree, one more day to play. And she didn't intend to waste a minute of it.

So she moved her hand under the covers, not stopping until she touched warm, smooth skin. Logan stirred and Peyton continued, cupping Logan's breast lightly, rubbing her nipple with her thumb. It became rigid immediately.

Logan opened her eyes, then pulled Peyton closer, rolling to her back. Peyton rested on top of her, their breasts touching as she leaned down for a kiss. The kiss deepened, their tongues dancing. Peyton moaned when Logan spread her thighs, and she pressed down into her. Logan's hands on her back nearly molded their bodies together as one. She pulled away from the kiss, breathing hard as they rocked together.

"Not yet," she whispered hoarsely, slowing their pace. She met Logan's stare. "I want you to use your mouth."

Logan's grin was almost wicked. "My pleasure," she murmured as she drew Peyton down for another kiss. "Why don't we both?"

Oh God.

"Turn around."

Peyton stared at her. It was once again something she had never done before. But considering everything they *had* done, she felt her embarrassment slip away as quickly as it had come. She nodded, doing as Logan requested.

Warm hands on her hips guided her back until she was straddling Logan's head. Peyton was literally trembling with anticipation as Logan lay sprawled out below her. She realized she was nearly panting and she tried to slow her breathing.

"Relax."

Oh God.

She had no more time to think as Logan pulled her hips down and she felt the quick brush of Logan's tongue. She moaned, then lowered her head, falling into Logan's wetness. She wrapped her lips around Logan's clit at the same instant Logan's mouth closed around hers. It was the most exquisite feeling in the world. She was almost delirious as they feasted on each other. Cognizant thoughts left her and all she held on to was the euphoric feeling that ran through her body. She was moaning loudly and couldn't help it. She no longer cared. She didn't know how close Logan was to orgasm, but she simply couldn't hold off any longer. Her world exploded in blinding colors as Logan's tongue continued its assault on her clit. Her mouth clamped down hard, sucking Logan's clit into her mouth, giving the last of her energy to Logan, hoping it was enough. She was rewarded with a guttural scream from Logan as her thighs tightened around her head.

Oh God.

She rolled to her side, resting her head against Logan's legs, trying to catch her breath. She couldn't keep the smile off her face. Damn, but that felt good.

"So, good morning," Logan said.

Peyton was too spent to raise her head, even though she recognized the amusement in Logan's voice.

"Thank you," was all she could manage.

Logan laughed quietly. "I think that should be a mutual thank you."

"God, that was awesome," she said.

Logan sat up and then reached for her. "Come back up here," she said.

Peyton finally moved, crawling back up the bed on her knees before falling down again. Letting Logan pull her closer, she laid her head against Logan's shoulder.

"Wonder what time it is?"

"I don't care," she said with a smile, letting her eyes close.

"Me either," Logan said.

Later, Peyton woke with a start, sitting up in bed. *Much* later, she assumed as sunlight streamed in through the opened blinds. Logan was nowhere to be found and a quick feel of the sheets told her she had been gone a while. She reached across the bed to the nightstand where her phone was. She was shocked to see that it was nearly noon. Although she didn't know why she was shocked. She was famished and the rumbling in her stomach reminded her so.

She got out of bed and looked for her clothes. They had left them strewn across the floor the night before. A quick glance around found them neatly folded on top of the dresser. She took them with her into the bathroom. She dressed quickly, deciding to go up to her own room to shower and put on clean clothes. She would decide then if she would get lunch or try to find Logan.

She felt a little self-conscious as she opened the door, taking a quick look around to see if anyone was watching. Of course, no one but she knew that she was sneaking out of another woman's room at noon. She skipped the elevator and used the stairs to the second floor. Her room was immaculate and she shook her head with a smile. In the last couple days, she'd hardly used it at all.

As hungry as she was, she'd planned a quick shower, but once she stood under the warm stream of water, she closed her eyes, standing there for long minutes before reaching for the soap. As she ran her slippery hands across her breasts, her thoughts immediately went to Logan. She hadn't had a lot of lovers in her life but certainly none of them had ever been as…well, as fantastic a lover as Logan was. She doubted she would ever find that again. Of course, maybe it was simply being a bit promiscuous on this vacation that made the sex seem fabulous.

Oh, well. She reminded herself—again—that she would be leaving in the morning. There was really no need to try to dissect the affair. She would enjoy the time that they had remaining and tuck the memories away to be enjoyed at a later date.

CHAPTER EIGHTEEN

Logan stopped by Emma's office before going in search of Peyton. She'd gone to get burgers at her favorite place and had picked up lunch for Emma as well.

"I've hardly seen you this trip," Emma complained as it was obvious Logan planned to eat elsewhere.

"Sorry, sis, but man, what a week it's been," she said with a grin.

"Did you get her name and address yet?"

Logan's smiled faltered. "No. She hasn't mentioned it. And she hasn't asked for mine either."

Emma shrugged. "Sorry, sweetie."

"Yeah. Oh well. It's been fun. But I need to head back in the morning. I promised Drew I'd help her on their pool house this weekend."

"You mean since you use it more than they do?"

"Yeah. I thought it was only right," she said with a laugh. "Their spring-fed pool is incredible and it's finally warm enough to use it again. But they're doing some renovations. There's an outdoor kitchen and whatnot." She held up the bag of burgers. "Got to go. I'll stop by and see you before I leave."

Emma shook her head. "I'm not working tomorrow. Natalie and I are taking a beach day down at Padre," she said.

"Then I'll catch you next trip." Emma stood up as Logan walked over and they hugged goodbye. "Thanks for putting me up. I had a fabulous time."

"You're welcome. I'll see you later."

"Love you."

"Love you too."

Logan stopped to take a peek at the pool, but she didn't really expect Peyton to be out there. She wasn't. Next, she stopped by her room. It was empty. So she headed to the stairs and hurried up to the second floor to Peyton's room. She knocked three times in quick succession, not even considering that Peyton might not be around.

But the door opened quickly and they stood there looking at each other, both smiling. Logan finally remembered the burgers and she held the bag up.

"Hungry?"

"God, yes," Peyton said as she drew her into the room. "I don't care what it is. I'll eat anything."

"Burgers and fries," Logan said, pulling a burger from the bag. "I got it with everything on it."

"Perfect," Peyton said, taking the burger. "It smells wonderful," she said as she nearly ripped the wrapping off.

"Figured you'd be hungry," Logan said. Her own stomach growled as she unwrapped hers.

"Starving," Peyton said before taking a bite. She moaned and closed her eyes as she chewed. "Very good," she mumbled.

Logan took a bite too. "It's a local joint," she explained after she swallowed. "Here. Fries."

They sat on the bed and laid the fries out between them. Logan tore into a packet of ketchup and squirted it all over her side of the fries. Peyton took one and dipped it into the ketchup, then nodded as Logan offered her a packet.

"What time did you get up?"

"Nearly noon," Peyton said. "I slept like a rock."

"No kidding. Even my singing in the shower didn't wake you," she said.

"I hate that I missed *that*," Peyton teased. "When did you leave?"

"About eleven thirty." Logan took another bite of her burger. "If you're feeling rested, I thought maybe we could do something fun today."

Peyton chewed slowly. "What did you have in mind?"

"Parasailing."

Peyton's eyes widened. "Parasailing?"

"Yeah. A buddy of mine owns a tour business. He would probably give us a break on the cost," she said.

Peyton put her burger down. "Parasailing?" she asked again. "Like flying over the water as if...well, like a kite?"

Logan laughed. "Yeah, kinda like a kite, I guess."

Peyton shook her head. "No. Absolutely not."

"Come on, Peyton. It'll be fun."

"Fun? You call that fun? Hanging by a thread over the Gulf?"

"It won't be out in the Gulf. He goes up Lydia Ann to Aransas Bay. There'll be land on both sides. You'll get a close-up of the old lighthouse. The views are great."

"I'll take your word for it," Peyton said as she picked up her burger again. "I'm not crazy about heights. In fact, it's all I can do to get on a plane."

"It's perfectly safe. You're in a harness. They wheel you out and back in. You don't even touch the water. Not like in the old days where you'd splash down. Now *that* was fun," she said.

"Well, I wouldn't mind a ride in the boat but getting up in the air, no."

"You can do two at a time," she said. "I'll be right there with you." She shrugged. "But if you don't want to, that's fine."

"Oh, no. We can go. I'll just watch."

"Great. Let me give him a call. You're going to love it. It'll be fun."

* * *

Peyton was enjoying the boat ride as they cruised up what she learned was the Lydia Ann Channel. Logan pointed out the deactivated lighthouse as they sped past. She saw something in the water and grasped Logan's arm excitedly. Two dolphins surfaced and then dove again.

"Did you see that?"

Logan smiled and nodded. "Yeah. Hopefully you'll get to see some more."

Logan's friend Brian had been between tours and had offered to take them out. He hadn't charged them yet, saying he would wait and see how long they were out. She had no clue what it cost to parasail or charter a boat, but Logan didn't seem concerned. Besides Brian, there were two crew members who would help Logan with the parasail. Peyton intended on taking pictures with her phone, nothing more. While she knew she wouldn't forget Logan, it would be nice to have a picture of her. It was only a plus that she was wearing her bikini, even though she had on water shorts too. They'd both worn T-shirts over their tops, and she, like Logan, had taken hers off as soon as they were on the boat.

As the channel widened, Peyton assumed they were now in Aransas Bay. The boat slowed, and Brian turned around, eyebrows raised.

"Ready?"

"You bet."

Logan looked at her. "You sure you don't want to try?"

"Very sure," she said.

"Okay. Wish me luck."

Logan surprised her by bending down for a kiss. Peyton was a bit embarrassed by such a public display, but no one seemed to have even noticed as the crew was readying the parasail.

Logan tightened her lifejacket and then slipped on the harness. Brian turned the boat slowly as the crew let out lines. Soon, the parasail was inflated and hanging overhead. It was a brightly colored sail with rainbow colors. Logan waved at her, then walked up on the launch deck. As the crew attached her harness to a bar, Peyton found her heart beating nervously. Logan had told her earlier that she would be two or three hundred feet in the air.

Logan gave a thumbs-up to Brian, who nodded and sped up. In a matter of seconds Logan was in the air. Peyton tried to take it all in, watching as a winch turned, giving Logan more line. She nearly forgot about taking pictures and quickly brought up her phone, but Logan was already too far away. The boat picked up speed, towing a waving Logan behind. Maybe ten minutes later, Brian slowed his pace and Peyton noticed the winch rewinding, pulling Logan back in. In no time, Logan landed safely on the deck, a huge smile on her face.

"God, that was awesome," she said excitedly as she stepped out of the harness. "You should try it."

And while it did look a lot safer than what she'd imagined, she still couldn't see herself dangling over the water like that.

"We can both go at the same time, you know."

Peyton hesitated. It *did* look like fun.

"I've been doing this a lot of years," Brian said. "Never had an accident even once."

"Come on. It'll be fun."

Peyton stared into Logan's eyes, wondering what it was about this woman that she could talk her into doing almost anything.

So she nodded. "Okay. I'll do it."

It was a whirlwind as she was fitted into her lifejacket and harness. She had no time to back out. Before she knew what was happening, she was sitting on the launch deck beside Logan, her harness clipped securely—she hoped—to the bar.

"Ready?"

"As I'll ever be," she said, taking a firm grip on the harness below the clip.

Logan gave thumbs-up, and Peyton braced herself for liftoff. It was so slight however, that she shouldn't have worried. The boat picked up speed, and they just floated away, sailing higher into the sky.

"Oh my God," she said. "It's like we're floating. I thought it would be really windy."

"It's not too bad. We're not going as fast as you think."

"Oh my God. We're getting higher," she said. "Should we be this high?"

"Relax. Enjoy the view."

That was easier said than done as a gust of wind blew against them. It was spectacular up this high, but she couldn't help but worry that the harness would hold, that the rope would hold.

"See the lighthouse?" Logan pointed. "The island is just past that. You can really see the channels from up here."

"Yes, but we're really, really high," she said, feeling a bit of vertigo as she looked down.

"You're doing great. Just relax. They'll bring us down in a minute."

Peyton felt a little more comfortable when Logan linked arms with her, pulling her closer. Peyton smiled her thanks and after taking a deep breath, she did indeed relax. As soon as she stopped worrying about the rope breaking and them plunging into the water, that is. Because, as Logan said, a few minutes later she felt the tug on the rope as they were being pulled back to the boat. She held tight to the harness as they approached the launch deck.

"Lift your legs up," Logan instructed.

Peyton did and they landed softly on the deck without incident. She let out a relieved breath, then broke into laughter.

"We made it!"

"Were you worried?" Logan asked as she helped her up.

"A little, yes." But she couldn't keep the smile from her face. "That was awesome." She looked up into the sky. "I mean, we were up there," she said, pointing. "I can't believe I just did that."

Logan unhooked her lifejacket, then helped Peyton with hers. "Unless you want to go again?"

"No, no. I'm good," she said with a laugh. She turned to Brian. "Thank you. That was fun."

"My pleasure."

Now that she was safely back in the boat, the whole thing seemed like no big deal. Of course, she doubted anyone from her real life would believe she'd just done that. That thought brought her back down to earth a bit. Her real life. She glanced at Logan, who turned, a smile on her face. Peyton returned it, although she was feeling a bit melancholy all of a sudden. She would be leaving tomorrow. Back to her real life. A life that did not include impromptu boat rides and parasailing. A life that was always regimented and planned, never spontaneous. And a life, certainly, that did not include Logan. God, how depressing.

Logan bumped her shoulder.

"You okay?"

Peyton nodded. "I guess it just hit me. Vacation is coming to an end."

Logan put an arm around her shoulder and pulled her close. "We still have one more night," she said directly into her ear. "Let's make it memorable."

Peyton laughed. "Can it get any better than last night?"

Logan laughed too. "Is that a challenge?"

* * *

Logan rolled onto her back, gasping for breath, wondering who was trying to kill whom. Peyton still clutched her hand tightly, and Logan smiled, doubting that it ever got any better than this.

"Don't ever do that again," Peyton said with short breaths.

"No? You did it to me first. And I thought you liked it."

"I did. I liked it a lot. But I'm still seeing stars."

Logan laughed quietly. "I'm thinking that's a good thing."

"Yeah. If you're *twenty*," Peyton said.

Logan laughed louder. "You're very flexible for your age."

Peyton groaned. "Please say that's not meant as a compliment."

Logan leaned over, trailing kisses along Peyton's stomach up to her breasts. "You have a fantastic body," she murmured. And apparently she couldn't get enough of it. Maybe it was because she knew their time together was dwindling, but she hadn't wanted to waste even one minute on sleeping. Thankfully, Peyton seemed to be of the same mind. She could only guess at the time but it had to be two or three in the morning by now.

"Come hold me," Peyton said quietly. "Let's rest."

Logan did as she was asked, spooning behind Peyton and wrapping her up tight in her arms. Peyton snuggled against her, their fingers entwining.

Logan wanted to stay awake, to savor these last few hours, but she felt herself getting drowsy. She couldn't remember the last time, if ever, she'd felt so wonderfully in tune with a lover. She and Peyton, for being practically strangers, had such great chemistry between them. It was a nice balance of give and take, something she wasn't used to. Most of the college girls she took to bed were more interested in receiving than giving, something she certainly didn't mind doing. But it was nice to have a lover who made sure Logan was equally satisfied. She sighed, thinking she'd never been more satisfied than she was at that moment. Her eyes slipped closed and she gave in to sleep…finally.

CHAPTER NINETEEN

Peyton wasn't exactly sure what the protocol was for saying goodbye to a woman she hardly knew, a woman she would never see again…yet physically, a woman she was *very* familiar with. The time spent with Logan had been more intimate—and intense—than any other time in her life. That included a nearly five-year relationship with Vicky. Never once had her lovemaking with Vicky even come close to what she and Logan shared. God, how sad was that?

Well, it would do her no good to dwell on it. Her luggage was packed, and she'd showered and put on clean clothes. Her flight was in three hours. She'd already called for a shuttle. Time to go home and get back to her real life. She hesitated, wondering why she was feeling so out of sorts this morning, wondering why she wished they'd have just one more day.

But they didn't. Logan was leaving as well. They'd already said their physical goodbyes. Even then, she had a hard time pulling out of Logan's arms, a hard time leaving her bed. One more kiss and then another. And she'd come so close to asking

Logan where she lived, so close to telling Logan where she lived. But in the end, she thought it would serve no purpose. While they enjoyed a holiday affair, it could never translate to the real world. And besides, if Logan wanted Peyton to know who she was, where she lived, she would have told her.

So they would meet for coffee as planned, say a final goodbye, then get on with their lives. A depressing prospect at the moment, but she was sure that after a few days, she would be able to put this whole affair into perspective. Namely, it was a fun adventure but one that was so out of character for her, she *still* had a hard time believing it.

She took one last glance around the room she had hardly used, pulled up the handle on her luggage and rolled it out into the hallway behind her.

She found Logan sitting at the bar as planned. She was dressed in army-green cargo shorts and a T-shirt advertising the Rainbow Island Resort. A gift from her sister, no doubt. She was holding a cup of coffee, and when Peyton approached, Logan held up her finger to the bartender, silently asking her to bring another cup.

"All packed?" Logan asked.

Peyton nodded. "You?"

"Yeah. It's already in my Jeep. I've got a painting gig this weekend," Logan said.

"Oh?" she asked as she stirred a little sugar into her coffee before taking a sip.

"Friends of mine are doing some renovations on their pool house. Since I like to sneak over there and use their pool, it seemed only right that I should volunteer my services," she said with a teasing smile.

That smile was yet one more thing that Peyton was sure to miss. Her own smile faded at the prospect. Logan seemed to read her mind. She reached out, taking her hand and entwining their fingers.

"It's been the best week, Peyton."

"Yes. It has." Then she allowed one more smile. "Thank you for stalking me."

Logan laughed. "Thank you for not calling the police."

They both let their smiles fade as their eyes held. Then one last squeeze of fingers and they let those too slip away.

"I should go," Peyton said. "The shuttle will be here any minute."

"You're flying out?"

"Yes."

Logan stood up and pulled Peyton up too. They embraced quickly—hard, tight—then they stepped apart, putting some space between them. There really wasn't anything left to say so Peyton simply nodded.

"Goodbye, Logan."

"Goodbye."

Peyton turned quickly, shocked by her sudden sense of loss. She hurried away, afraid that if she turned around to look at Logan even once she'd run back into her arms. Thankfully, the shuttle pulled up in front of the resort as soon as she got there. She turned back then, glancing behind her, but Logan wasn't there watching her. That was just as well, she told herself.

* * *

"Damn," Logan whispered as Peyton rounded the corner, out of sight. She hadn't expected it to be so hard watching Peyton walk out of her life. She tossed a few dollars on the bar, then headed to her Jeep. So it was over with. Just like that.

Even though it was plenty warm out, she took the top off the Jeep. There was no better way to clear her head than a three-hour drive in the sunshine and wind. But before she started out, she picked up her phone, calling Emma.

"Yeah, sorry to bother you on your day off," she said.

"We just got out here," Emma said. "You heading back to Austin?"

"Yeah." She paused. "Peyton just left. You didn't tell me she flew in."

"And?"

"So if she flew, does that mean she doesn't live in Texas?"

"I take it she still didn't share anything with you?"

Logan blew out her breath. "No. Nothing."

"I'm sorry."

"And you're still not going to tell me?"

"Come on, Logan. Like I said, if she wanted you to know—"

"She would have told me," Logan finished for her. "I know. You're right."

"So you really liked this woman, huh? She's a little old for you, isn't she?" Emma asked with a laugh.

Logan laughed too. "Maybe I'm growing up."

"About time."

"Yeah, yeah." She looked up into the clear sky, watching as a few puffy clouds drifted in from the Gulf. "Okay. You two girls have fun on the beach. I'll probably come back in September, after the crowds thin out a bit."

"Okay, sis. Drive carefully."

"I will."

She started her Jeep, then took one last look at the resort, knowing she could never come back here without Peyton being in her every thought.

"Damn."

CHAPTER TWENTY

Peyton sat at her desk, her chin resting in the palm of her hand, staring absently out the window. The office space they rented was a cute, older building that housed only them and a law firm. Two of the attorneys were young, outdoorsy types who rode bikes to work every day. They'd also fixed up the back, making a patio and a sitting area. Two bird feeders and a birdbath for water were placed next to the trees along the fence. While they had done all the work, they'd offered the sitting area for Peyton and her staff to use as well. She knew the others used it on occasion, but she had never once set foot out there. But for some reason ever since she'd gotten back from her vacation she longed to sit in the shade and watch the birds at the feeder. So far, she had resisted.

"Are you ready to talk yet?"

Peyton jerked her head around, surprised to find Susan standing by her desk. She hadn't heard her come in.

"Talk?"

Susan must have taken that as a "yes" and plopped down in the visitor's chair. "You've been back over a month now. Or someone who looks like you has been back over a month."

Peyton gave her a humorless smile. She knew she had been noncommittal about her trip, giving only cursory details. "Yes, it was very relaxing. Yes, I had a great time." Not much more than that. She thought it was enough.

"What's going on with you, Peyton? You hardly talk to anyone. You sit and stare out the window most of the day. I'm assuming you're taking work home since you don't seem to be backlogged," Susan said.

Peyton arched an eyebrow. "You do know I am still the boss, right?"

Susan brushed her protest away with a wave of her hand. "We both know I run the office," she said with a smile. "Now tell me what's going on with you. I've never seen you this way."

Peyton knew she was right. "Do you know Margot Joseph?"

"I know the name. She's an attorney. I've seen her commercials."

"Yes. And you know how I feel about attorneys." She paused. "She's invited me to dinner."

Susan's eyes lit up. "Like a date? That's great. It's about time."

"It is, I suppose," she agreed.

"Why does that have you in a funk?" Susan paused. "Please don't say it has something to do with Vicky. Not after all this time."

"No. God, no," Peyton said with a shake of her head. "It has to do with Logan."

Susan frowned. "Who is Logan?"

Peyton had vowed she would never tell anyone about Logan, about their affair. Once she was back in her familiar surroundings, she was even more taken aback over her actions. It was so unlike her, so out of character for her, that she was doubly embarrassed by the whole thing. That, of course, didn't stop her from hoping Logan would pop back into her life one day. She knew if Logan really wanted to see her, really wanted to contact her, all she had to do was to get her personal information from her sister. As each day passed, and then each week, without contact, she was more convinced than ever that their time together was simply what she'd thought all along—a holiday affair, nothing more.

She ran into Margot at her come-and-go birthday happy hour last week. She'd met her before but had never spoken more than a few words to her. That evening, they spent nearly an hour chatting, and before she knew it, Margot had invited her to dinner. Peyton had been flattered that Margot had asked. Margot was attractive and quite popular among their circle of friends. She hadn't accepted, however. She asked Margot to call her next week—this week—and she had. This time, Peyton accepted. They were going out tomorrow night.

She looked at Susan. "You think I should go, right?"

"Wait a minute. Who is Logan?"

"I met her when I was on vacation," she said.

"And what does she have to do with Margot Joseph?"

Peyton bit her lip. "I kinda…I kinda had an affair with her."

Susan jumped out of her chair, her eyes wide. "What? *You?*" Susan shook her head. "You don't have affairs."

"Oh, God, I know. It was so…*so* not me," she admitted. "But it was so wonderful," she added with a smile.

"Okay, so you had an affair. I mean, like sex and everything?"

"Lots of sex," Peyton said, feeling a blush on her face. "A…a lot."

"Oh my *God*!" Susan nearly shrieked. "With a stranger you just met? Are you insane?"

"It's your fault," Peyton said, pointing at her. "You made me go. You said to relax. To recharge."

"I didn't say to grab the first woman you saw and sleep with her." Then Susan grinned. "So it was wonderful, huh?"

"I've never been flirted with so shamelessly in my entire life. And she was young and cute and fun and I just…went with it."

"How young?"

"We celebrated her thirtieth birthday," she said.

"That's not so young. I thought you were going to say twenty or something."

"Thirty is young when you consider the women I hang around with. Margot, for instance. She's at least ten years older than I am."

Susan sat down again. "So you've been in a funk ever since you got back. Is it because of this woman? Logan?"

"I don't know. I'm just having a hard time getting back into the swing, I guess. We never exchanged last names. I have no idea where she lives. Yet I find myself thinking about her all the time. I miss her," she admitted. "I miss her smile and her laughter. I miss being with her."

"Fine. But what does this have to do with Margot? Logan was an affair. She's not here. Margot is. I think you should go out with her, get on with your life."

"I know."

Yes, she needed to just let Logan go, forget about her. She would never forget about the affair, of course. That was something etched in her mind forever. But Susan was right. She needed to get on with her life. When she looked back on this, she would remember her vacation as a jumpstart to the rest of her life. At least, she hoped she would. Starting to date again was the first step.

She smiled at Susan. "We're going to dinner tomorrow night."

"Good. And I'm not sure she's ten years older than you are. She looks good in those commercials."

Peyton nodded. Yes, Margot Joseph was very attractive. She had a very successful business, but really, she was nothing more than an ambulance chaser. Of course, her disdain for attorneys had more to do with Vicky and her current love interest than it did with Margot. But the circle got smaller, and she would just *die* if she ran into Vicky while they were out.

Her life seemed much less complicated while she was at the beach. Of course, vacations were supposed to have that effect on a person. Having hot sex and a lot of it surely didn't hurt matters.

Oh, yeah. She was supposed to *stop* thinking about Logan, wasn't she?

CHAPTER TWENTY-ONE

Logan grabbed a pepperoni off the top of the pizza as Jay brought it to the table. A ceiling fan circled overhead and another fan blew on them from the corner. July was not normally the best time to have dinner outside, but they'd finally finished with the pool house and all three had wanted to enjoy it. They'd spent nearly an hour in the pool before succumbing to hunger.

Drew held up her beer bottle, clicking lightly on hers. "Thanks for all your help."

"My pleasure," Logan said.

And it was. She'd first met Drew and Jay four years ago when they'd all been contracted out on the same house. Drew, with her organic landscaping business, and Jay, who was just making a name for herself in her design business, and Logan, who had made an appearance before making a bid on the painting—they had hit it off immediately, even though Drew and Jay were a little older than she was. It wasn't long before Logan was spending nearly as much time with them, here at their house, as she was at her own apartment. Drew's grandfather had built the place and

Drew had remodeled the house a couple of times, but it was the pool and garden that had the most appeal. The S-shaped, spring-fed pool was all limestone and slate rocks and the trees, shrubs and flowers surrounding it on all sides made for a near-jungle feel to it. Of course, what made it all the better—Drew was a fan of skinny-dipping too.

"You've been helping us nearly every weekend," Jay said. "And not once have you brought one of your college girls around." She took a bite of her pizza. "What's up with that?"

"Do you miss them?"

Jay shook her head. "I was nearly fifteen years older than the last one you brought around. I hardly knew what to say to her."

"Courtney? Yeah, she was young. Drew was old enough to be her mother," she teased.

Drew laughed good-naturedly. "I'm telling you, forty is no big deal. Jay is right behind me."

"Thanks for reminding me."

Logan laughed with them. "I won't have a problem turning forty. Thirty was pretty fantastic. I can only hope forty is the same."

It was Jay who leaned closer with a curious expression on her face. "And why was that? You've been very vague about your time down at the coast."

Logan shrugged. She wasn't sure why she hadn't mentioned Peyton to them. Maybe because she wanted to keep Peyton all to herself.

"Well, there was a woman," she said.

"A woman?" Jay asked.

"Closer to your age, actually. She's thirty-five."

"Wow. That must be a first for you."

Logan nodded. "Yeah. We had a...*really* good time. But it didn't go past that. I don't even know where she's from."

"Well, I suppose that at least told you that you could have fun with a more mature woman. Maybe you'll stop ogling the college students now," Jay said with a smile. "Don't you think it's time you settled down?"

"You sound like Emma," Logan said. "And when I was in my twenties, it didn't seem odd that I was dating college girls." She shrugged again. "Now? Well, maybe you're right." She grinned. "But damn, they've got stamina."

"It's the quality, not the quantity," Jay said. "Besides, Drew and I still have plenty of stamina."

Logan laughed when Drew actually blushed. "Can we change the subject?" Drew asked. "How about we discuss the party?"

The "party" was their annual get-together for their new clients as well as some of the builders they did business with. Logan had made a lot of contacts at these gatherings. She was looking forward to this year's event as well. The first two they'd held here at the house, but they had quickly outgrown that. They now rented a place and had it catered.

"I thought you'd decided on barbeque again," Logan said.

"We're thinking more of finger foods and a buffet. You can mingle better that way," Jay said. "If everyone's at a designated table with a full meal, it's hard to make the rounds and talk business."

"Sandwiches? Cheese and crackers? What?"

"A little fancier than just that," Drew said. "Smoked turkey or brisket."

"We could still do a barbeque theme," Jay said. "We could just do mini-sandwiches instead of a full meal. We could have different tables set up, all with different combinations of food. That way, guests can make the rounds to each table and still be able to mingle."

"Margarita machine?" Logan asked hopefully.

Drew shook her head. "Beer and wine only."

"We're shooting for mid-August again," Jay said. "Does that suit you?"

"Of course. I wouldn't miss it."

"I hope your college girls will be back in town by then. I'd hate for you to actually have to work to get a date," she said with a laugh.

"Me? Work?"

No, Peyton was really the only time she had to work at it. Logan had had several opportunities to go out these last six or eight weeks, but she hadn't been in the mood. In fact, every time she thought about asking someone out, Peyton popped into her mind and she just lost interest. But hell, it had been long enough. She'd met a graduate student, a friend of a friend. She was cute, she was blonde and she had made it clear she was interested. Staci would do nicely to get her back into the swing of things. In fact, she might borrow Ted's boat and ask her out to the lake. She suspected she would look hot in a bikini.

CHAPTER TWENTY-TWO

Peyton nodded at the appropriate times, trying really, really hard to appear interested in what Margot was telling her. A parking brake didn't hold, someone tried to keep the car from rolling back by pushing it, messed up their knee, surgery, made a lot of money. Even the guy who had to have surgery made a little. To hear Margot talk, she'd pocketed most of it.

"I love cases like that," Margot continued. "Easy. Cut and dried. The insurance company had no choice."

Peyton smiled and nodded politely. "I guess not." She sipped from her wineglass as Margot launched into another story. It was their second date. Dinner out again. The restaurant was nice, one Peyton had been to before. It turned out Margot was a bit of a wine connoisseur, even speaking French to the waiter as she selected a bottle. At one time, Peyton would have been thoroughly impressed by that. Tonight, though, she felt it was staged and all for show. As Margot continued her monologue, Peyton had to remind herself that she was lucky to be out with Margot. Margot was a dark-haired beauty and considered to be a good catch. She reminded herself that some of her friends were quite jealous that they were dating.

Of course, she wasn't certain she would call it dating. Their second date came almost a month after their first. And the first had ended with a quick kiss on the cheek, nothing more. In fact, because of that, Peyton had been shocked that Margot had actually called and asked her out again.

"I'd like for you to see it."

Peyton blinked several times, wondering what it was Margot was talking about. She *really* needed to pay better attention.

"Of course, I'll wait until I'm moved in," Margot said with a quick laugh. "I'll probably have a small get-together. I spent that much money, I should really show it off."

Oh. Her new house. The custom-built house that was "fabulous" and "cost a fortune." The house that had taken nearly a year to complete. Peyton smiled and nodded.

"I'll look forward to it. It sounds quite remarkable."

"Oh, it is. I lucked out on the designer too. I was going to go with Wilkes and Bonner," Margot said. "They're the biggest in Austin and most of the custom builders use them. But I just didn't get a good feel when I interviewed them. I went with Jay Burns instead. She's really talented. And quite attractive," she said with a laugh. "But her partner owns Montgomery Landscaping. All organic, which is a plus. I ended up using both of them and I couldn't be happier."

"Yes, I've actually used Montgomery Landscaping myself," Peyton said.

"Really? Well, maybe you'd like to accompany me to their party."

"What party?"

"They have a yearly party, a thank-you of sorts, I suppose. They invite their most current clients. I hadn't heard of it before, but I did some inquiring. Apparently, all the major builders show up." Margot smiled again. "I feel obligated to go. I mean, I'm so pleased with their work."

Peyton nodded. "Of course."

"It's next Saturday. Seven. Interested?"

Peyton wondered how rude it would be to say no, she wasn't interested in the least. But her social life was nearly nonexistent. Besides going out with Margot, she'd had lunch a few times with friends and had been on three blind dates, all of which were forgettable. She wouldn't say disastrous, but she knew within the first five minutes of each that she would never go out with any of them again. To make matters worse, one of them actually was friends with Vicky and her new partner. Talk about awkward. So now she plastered a smile on her face and nodded with as much enthusiasm as she could muster.

"I'd love to go."

"Great." Margot smiled at her, then reached across the table and took her hand. "Listen, after dinner, do you want to go do something fun?"

Peyton nodded. "Sure. It's still early," she said.

"I've got tickets to the lecture series at the university. Tonight's lecture is on urban development and modern architecture. When I started in college, that was my dream."

"To lecture?"

"No," Margot laughed. "To be an architect. I would have made a good one."

"I'm sure you would have."

Peyton tried not to choke on her wine as she contemplated a "fun" evening sitting through a lecture on architecture. The only thing she could think of that would be worse would be a trip to the dentist for a root canal.

Later, as she was seated next to Margot in the plush theater, the lights just dark enough for them to remain anonymous in the crowd, she took the time to reflect on her feelings at that moment—her true inner feelings. She was shocked to admit to herself that what she was feeling, right then, right there, was depression. Not the depression of despair or hopelessness. Rather, a deep unhappiness settled over her. So much so that she wanted to curl into a ball and cry. That shocked her even more. She was *not* a crier. She glanced over at Margot, noting her rapt attention on the speaker. Margot looked at her briefly and smiled, then turned back to the stage.

Peyton wasn't entirely sure what was wrong with her. Margot was exactly her type. She was a professional woman, she was well established, she was stable. And she was attractive to boot. They also had a number of mutual friends, which was always a bonus. Unfortunately, there wasn't even a hint of a spark between them. At least as far as Peyton was concerned. But perhaps she was being too hasty. This was only their second date.

She sighed, longing for the night to be over with. She wanted to go home, slip into some comfortable clothes…and be depressed all alone rather than in a room full of strangers.

CHAPTER TWENTY-THREE

Logan led Staci through the crowd, wondering why in the world she'd let herself be talked into going to a bar at this hour of the night. She'd had a busy day at work, and she would have another busy one tomorrow. When she'd invited Staci out to dinner, she thought they would get to know each other better, maybe make plans for a second date. Staci was in her first year of graduate school and seemed a little more mature than most. But after dinner, just as Logan was about to suggest she take her home, Staci had suggested the bar instead. At the time, Logan imagined them dancing. She hadn't missed the fact that Staci wore no bra. Maybe their first date might turn out to be more than just dinner after all. But now as she tried to find a spot at a table, the crowd loud and boisterous around her, she forgot all about Staci's lack of a bra.

"Kinda crowded," she said loudly. "Sure you want to do this?"

Staci grabbed her hips and pulled Logan close to her. "Let's get a drink or two first. Then we'll do it," she said with a laugh.

Okay, then. So maybe she'd be late to work tomorrow.

After her second drink, Staci made it perfectly clear that she meant what she said. Her dancing was nothing if not suggestive, and Logan found herself responding to her. However, a short time later, when Staci had Logan pinned against the wall by the restrooms—her tongue shoved in her mouth—Logan knew it was time to leave.

"How about we take this somewhere else?" she said between kisses.

"My place?"

"Sure."

It was a quick but challenging drive as Staci was practically in her lap, hands roaming her body at will.

"God, you're hot," Staci said into her ear. "I like an older woman who knows what she's doing."

Logan laughed. "Well, I know what I'm doing. Don't know about the 'older' part, though."

Once inside Staci's apartment, it was all a whirlwind. Staci ripped her own blouse off, confirming Logan's claim that she wore no bra. Staci's hands then went to Logan's jeans, unbuttoning them quickly.

"My bedroom's a mess," Staci said. "How about the sofa?"

"Whatever," Logan said as she kicked her jeans off.

She hardly had time to step out of them before Staci pulled her down to the couch. As Logan lay on top of her, it occurred to her how slight Staci was, how young she was. She shook those thoughts away as her hand moved between them. She might be young, but she was no child. Her thighs parted invitingly, and Logan went there, finding her wet and ready. She closed her eyes as she entered her, trying to wipe away the image of Peyton lying beneath her.

"Oh, yeah. Harder," Staci panted. "Do me harder."

Logan did.

CHAPTER TWENTY-FOUR

Peyton twirled her pencil between her fingers, her gaze fixed again on the bird feeders outside her office window. They'd been there for over a year but it was only recently that she even took notice of them. Maybe because it was only recently that she found herself staring outside…daydreaming.

Daydreaming of her toes in the warm sand, the gulf breeze in her hair, the sounds of laughing gulls and splashing surf. And envisioning a moon—a midnight moon—overhead. Envisioning sunshine and clear, blue skies. And Logan there beside her, her flirty smile, her sensuous lips. Her body glistening, the bikini hiding little. Then later, that bikini slipping off her body, revealing—

She stopped her thoughts before they could go any further. She'd done a good job of putting Logan from her mind these past few months. But since she'd started dating again, since she'd been out with Margot—since Margot had kissed her so passionately the other night—thoughts of Logan had returned. Because she felt absolutely nothing with any of these other women. Margot's passionate kiss stirred nothing in her. Yet she went along with it. She let Margot's hands travel up her waist, she let Margot touch her breast. It was only when she realized exactly what Margot had in mind that she slowed things down, telling Margot "not yet."

"Stuck?"

Peyton turned, offering a quick smile to Susan. "No. I'm finished with the account," she said. She tossed her pencil down. "She wants to sleep with me."

Susan's eyebrows shot up. "Mrs. Sharper?" she asked, referring to the account Peyton had been working on.

Peyton laughed. "No. Margot Joseph."

Susan sat down. "And that's a bad thing?"

"I'm not sure it's a good idea. We've only been out twice."

"Good Lord, Peyton. On vacation, you slept with a woman you'd just met."

"I know I did. Do you think I've forgotten?"

"Well? Then what's wrong with Margot?"

"Nothing's wrong with her. Well, other than she's an ambulance chaser," she said. "She's perfect for me, really. She's exactly my type. Right?"

"Yes. Or so you say."

Peyton groaned and banged her head lightly on her desk. "I know." She lifted her head up. "I don't even know what my type is anymore. After dinner the other night, we went to a lecture. I was bored out of my mind. I wanted to be anywhere but there."

"So why did you go?"

"She wanted to do something fun," Peyton said.

"Fun? A lecture?"

"I know. And I shouldn't judge. I mean, Vicky liked to go to lectures. We went before. A lot of my friends go."

Susan shrugged. "So sleep with her. See how it goes."

"That's just it. I'm not really attracted to her," she said. "I don't think it's going to *go* very well."

"But you're going out again?"

Peyton nodded. "Saturday night. Something else I don't want to go to. Her designer or something is having a party for their clients," she said with a wave of her hand. "Probably a bunch of snooty rich people comparing blueprints of their custom homes."

Susan laughed. "You have a custom home," she reminded her.

"Yes, but it's not *my* custom home," she said. "I never would have built it with four bedrooms."

"So are you going with her?"

"I don't know. I keep hoping I'll come down with the flu or something."

CHAPTER TWENTY-FIVE

Peyton had no such luck with the flu, and she walked beside Margot, feeling slightly overdressed. Margot had assumed it was a dressy affair and they both wore business suits. However, judging by the other guests, it was much more of a casual party. And why not? It was a Saturday evening in August. Peyton looked with envy at a woman wearing light khaki pants and a cool, sleeveless shirt. The first thing she planned to do was to ditch the jacket, at least.

"They have wine," Margot said. "I'll bring you a glass."

"Okay, thanks."

As soon as Margot left her, she slipped out of her suit jacket and draped it over her arm. There appeared to be an odd mix of guests, some wearing jeans and some slacks, but she did see a few other women with suits on so she didn't feel quite as conspicuous as before. She glanced around the room, wondering how long Margot would want to stay. Then she heard laughter to her left, a hauntingly familiar laugh, and she turned toward it.

Oh my God.

The woman had her back to her but still, Peyton actually had to remind herself to breathe again. Could it possibly be?

Oh my God. She blinked several times, wondering if she were dreaming. Surely it couldn't be. Then the woman turned, as if feeling Peyton watching her.

Logan. Their eyes held, and she recognized the shock in Logan's gaze. She was certain hers looked the same. Then Logan smiled—that sexy, flirty smile that Peyton would always remember—and headed toward her. Logan was dressed casually in jeans and a polo shirt and she looked as attractive—and irresistible—as she remembered. She hesitated only a heartbeat before going to Logan. They embraced quickly, and Peyton felt a myriad of emotions in those few seconds that they held each other.

"What in the world are you doing here?" Logan asked with a grin.

"I could ask you the same thing," Peyton said.

"You live here? In Austin?" Peyton nodded and Logan's laughter rang out. "What are the chances?"

Peyton couldn't keep the smile off her face. "You too?"

"Yeah. Well, not in the city, but close enough." Logan stared into her eyes. "You look…you look great, Peyton."

Peyton shrugged. "We thought it was more formal."

Logan arched an eyebrow. "We?"

Peyton smiled almost apologetically. "A…a friend," she said. Then she turned, seeing Margot approach. Suddenly, everything seemed far too complicated and she wondered why she felt guilty. Was it for Logan's sake or Margot's?

"There you are," Margot said, pausing to glance only briefly at Logan. "There's someone I want you to meet."

"Of course." Peyton turned back to Logan. "Well, I guess—"

"Yeah, sure," Logan said. "Go on. Maybe we'll get a chance to chat later."

Peyton nodded, wondering if that was a good idea or not. Her heart was pounding nervously as it was and she took Margot's hand. *Oh my God.* She couldn't believe Logan was here, of all places. She chanced a quick glance behind her, seeing Logan return to the people she'd been talking to. The young blonde woman instantly linked arms with Logan and Peyton felt a stab of jealousy. She pulled her eyes away and tightened her grip on Margot's hand.

"This is the woman who designed the interior of my home," Margot was saying and Peyton pulled her thoughts back to the present. "Jay Burns."

Peyton shook her hand politely. She appeared to be near her own age, maybe a little older. Jay's hair was blonde, a little darker than her own, and she had friendly blue eyes. Peyton matched her smile.

"Glad you could make it," Jay said.

"Her partner, Drew, owns the landscaping company that designed my yard and pool area," Margot said. "Of course, you actually had Montgomery do work for you too."

"A few years ago, yes," Peyton said.

"Well, Jay, I must say, the house turned out fabulous. Thank you. When I envisioned the blended color scheme on the walls, I was afraid you wouldn't be able to pull it off, but they're magnificent."

Jay laughed lightly. "I didn't know if we could pull it off either," she said. "But I can't take credit for the work. All I did was design the color scheme. The painting was done by Weaver Painting Pros." She looked around. "In fact, I know Logan is here somewhere. She owns the company."

Peyton's breath caught. Surely there was only one Logan here. Apparently, their world was getting smaller by the minute. And she *owned* the company? She slowly shook her head, remembering their conversation that day on the beach about Logan's profession—a painter.

"There she is," Jay said. "Let me get her. She's very nice. You'll love her."

Margot leaned closer as Jay walked toward Logan. "Isn't that the woman you were chatting with earlier?"

"Yes. Small world, isn't it?"

But Logan's smile was infectious, and Peyton returned it as Logan walked over with Jay. Jay motioned between them.

"This is Margot Joseph. We finished our part of her house nearly a month ago," Jay said.

Logan and Margot shook hands, then Logan motioned to Peyton.

"Actually, Peyton and I met earlier this summer," Logan explained. "Down in Port Aransas."

"I was on vacation," Peyton added quickly, wondering why she felt compelled to explain.

"Oh? So this is the one—"

"Yes," Logan said quickly, cutting Jay off.

"Oh," Margot said, smiling between the two of them. "Well, I just wanted to thank you personally," she said. "The color blends. Absolutely fabulous."

Logan nodded. "I remember the house," she said. "It was a challenge. We don't normally blend that many colors, but it turned out nicely."

"Logan's company is the best," Jay said. "And I don't say that just because we're friends," she added with a smile, then glanced beyond them. "Oh, there's Randy Kline. I've got to visit with him. He gave me my first job about five years ago." She shook Margot's hand. "Glad you could make it, Margot." She nodded at Peyton. "I hope you enjoy the party."

"Thank you."

"See you later," Logan said to Jay.

The three of them stood there a bit awkwardly, and Peyton was searching for something to say when Margot cleared her throat.

"I never did get to the bar. Let me see if I can finally find us a glass of wine." She glanced at Logan. "Give you two a chance to visit." She raised her eyebrows. "Wine?"

"No thanks," Logan said, holding up a beer bottle. "I'm fine."

As soon as she was gone, Logan took her arm and led her away to a more private spot to talk.

"So, a painter, huh?" Peyton began. "You didn't tell me you owned the business."

Logan shrugged. "I also paint. Sometimes. When they let me," she laughed. "But my father still technically owns the business. He just spends more time at the lake fishing than he does painting. So it's my business to run."

"And here I envisioned you in white pants and shirt, maybe a painter's hat too," Peyton said with a quiet laugh.

"Did you envision me with those clothes on or off?" Logan teased.

Peyton blushed immediately. "Actually, on," she lied. She thought it was safer than the truth. "So, out with one of your college girls? She looks very young."

Logan nodded. "Yeah, she's twenty-two, twenty-three, maybe. Grad student."

"Wow." So this is who Logan normally dated. The girl was more than ten years younger than Peyton. Logan leaned closer, her gaze holding Peyton's.

"Yes, she's a twenty-something college student. You're a thirty-five-year-old woman."

Peyton shook her head. "If that's supposed to be a compliment, it's not very flattering," she said.

"Of course it's a compliment," Logan said. "And you should be flattered. I've seen you both naked."

Again, a stab of jealousy hit. "Yes, I suppose you are sleeping with her. Who wouldn't?"

"I never said I was sleeping with her. I just said I've seen her naked." She wiggled her eyebrows. "There are a number of ways to do that, you know. Skinny-dipping, for instance."

At that, Peyton laughed. "Skinny-dipping is still a favorite pastime, I see."

Logan's smiled faded slightly. "So? You and Margot Joseph. Is it serious?"

Peyton shook her head. "No. Just the third date."

Logan's smile returned. "Third date, huh? That's the sex date, right?"

Peyton frowned. "What do you mean?"

"You know, the first, you get to know each other. The second, a little kissing, just to test the waters. And third? Dive right in."

"Is that your dating philosophy?"

"No, I don't really follow that outline."

"No, I don't suppose you do," Peyton said. "But I enjoy her company. I don't know what's going to come of it." Was that a lie? Did she enjoy Margot's company?

"Well, she's practically a celebrity," Logan said. "I see her commercials all the time. In fact—"

But Logan was cut off as Margot returned with two wineglasses and a bottle of beer. She handed the beer to Logan.

"I thought you'd be empty by now."

"Thank you. I am." Logan glanced around her. "I guess I should go rescue Staci. I left her with a couple of builders. All they were doing was staring at her breasts." She held her hand out to Margot. "Great to meet you finally. Glad my guys did a nice job on your house."

"Yes, thank you. They did."

Logan turned to her, meeting her eyes briefly. "Peyton, good to see you again. Take care."

Peyton nodded, hating the formality between them, wondering if this was the last she would see of Logan. But there was nothing she could do. Not with Margot standing there looking at her expectantly. So she offered her hand to Logan, relishing the quick touch of her fingers, the gentle squeeze.

"You too," she said and even managed a slight smile. And then Logan was gone, off to find Staci and her breasts. *God, I hate my life.*

"She was nice," Margot offered. "Cute."

"Yes."

"Did you get a look at her date? Wow."

Yes, wow indeed. But she intentionally kept her gaze away from Logan thereafter, instead following Margot around like a puppy dog, meeting more people than she could possibly remember names for and stopping off not once, but twice at the buffet table. After her fourth glass of wine, she decided she'd had enough, especially when she found her arm linked with Margot's. She was sending a signal for something she wasn't sure she was ready for or even wanted.

But as they were leaving, she spied Logan and her date, and her eyes were drawn to the fingers that were playing upon

Logan's arm, fingers that seemed to be dancing on her skin. She turned away quickly, letting Margot take her hand. So the third date was the sex date, huh? Well, why not?

Of course, by the time they got to her house, she nearly talked herself out of it, despite the fact that Margot's hand had been resting on—and rubbing—her thigh during the drive.

"May I come in?" Margot asked suggestively.

Peyton hesitated—*oh, God*—then nodded. "Yes. Come inside."

She supposed she'd had just enough wine to numb her senses, but not enough to totally disengage from what she was doing. Margot's kiss was gentle at first, then deepened. Peyton tried to feel something, she really did. But she found herself going through the motions, touching Margot without really thinking, feeling disjointed. They undressed slowly and she was surprised that Margot actually took the time to fold her clothes neatly. God, with Logan, they had ripped their clothes off and tossed them down without thought. And with thoughts of Logan came thoughts of the young blonde. Was Logan with her right now? Was she touching her?

"You have a fantastic body," Margot murmured as her hand touched her breast lightly. "Do you run?"

Peyton shook her head. "I swim."

Margot pulled her close, their bodies touching for the first time. "I have a pool, but I don't really like to swim," she said as she trailed kisses along her neck. "Maybe you can change that."

Oh, God, what am I doing, she thought as Margot lowered her head, her tongue raking across her nipple. But it was too late to back out now. She let Margot guide her to the bed, praying arousal would come. She squeezed her eyes shut, picturing another woman touching her, another woman's mouth at her breasts. Only then did she open to Margot, only then did she feel her pulse race. But no matter how much she wanted to pretend, it still wasn't Logan touching her, it wasn't Logan making love to her. And when Margot reached orgasm, Peyton was still so far away. She did what she swore she would never do. She faked her climax. Margot seemed pleased with herself and gathered Peyton closer even though all Peyton wanted to do was to pull out of her arms and put an end to the evening. To her horror, Margot fell asleep and Peyton let out a heavy sigh, her eyes glued to the ceiling, hating herself at that moment. She had a passionate ache for someone and it wasn't Margot.

God, I hate my life.

CHAPTER TWENTY-SIX

"Not tonight," Logan said as Staci tried to pull her inside her apartment. She gently untangled herself from Staci, not wanting to hurt her feelings. Staci had made it perfectly clear she wanted to have sex.

"What's wrong? I thought you had a good time the other night?"

"Oh, I did. It was great," she said. "I've got to help a friend out very early in the morning." Then she rubbed her temple. "And I have a touch of a headache," she added, hoping she sounded convincing.

"That's not fair, Logan. I sat through your boring party for nothing then."

"Boring? You got free dinner and booze," she said.

"Like I couldn't get that anytime I wanted," Staci said with a toss of her blonde hair. "If you're not interested, I'll just go to the bar then."

Logan didn't know if she was saying that hoping to get a jealous reaction or what, and frankly, she didn't care.

"Great. But be careful. You've been drinking."

"Yes. I've been drinking and I want to have sex," Staci said, rubbing her hand up Logan's chest.

Logan stopped her movements before she reached her breast. "I'm sorry. But I need to go."

"Fine." Staci closed her door and locked it. "I'm going out."

Logan stepped aside as Staci brushed past her and headed to her car. Logan shook her head as she stood there by Staci's apartment, watching as she sped away. She blew out her breath, wondering if she should have just taken her to bed and gotten it over with.

But no. It wasn't Staci she wanted. It wasn't this twenty-something college girl she wanted to be with.

She headed toward her Jeep, trying not to think about Peyton with Margot Joseph. Were they in bed now? Were they touching? Were Margot's hands on her body, on her breasts?

Images of her and Peyton came flooding back. It felt like only yesterday that they were down at the coast…playing, laughing, making love. She remembered the feel of Peyton's skin. She remembered how dark Peyton's blue eyes got when she entered her. She remembered how it felt to have Peyton's nipple in her mouth, the taste of her, and God, the sound she made as she climaxed. She remembered it all like it was yesterday.

And now here they were. What were the chances that they'd run into each other? She had convinced herself that she would never see Peyton again. She'd tried twice more to get Emma to give up her information, but each time, Emma had refused. Logan had finally accepted it. Peyton would be a memory, nothing more. But here she was, living in Austin. And dating Margot Joseph. Margot was an attorney. She was a professional woman. A very successful professional woman, judging by the home she'd had custom built. She was someone who Peyton had professed was exactly her type. Logan couldn't even begin to compete with Margot Joseph.

She needed to just let it go. Peyton hadn't given her any indication that she wanted to see her again. In fact, it was almost like Peyton had gone out of her way to avoid her at the party. Yeah, she would let it go. After all, Peyton wasn't her type. No,

Staci was her type. Staci, the young college student who wanted to have sex with her. Staci, the one who had run off to the bar because Logan *didn't* want to have sex with her.

What is wrong with you?

CHAPTER TWENTY-SEVEN

"Hello? Earth to Peyton."

Peyton turned away from the window, staring blankly at Susan.

"I said, do you want to have lunch?"

Peyton frowned. "Us?"

"Yes."

"You've worked for me for over eight years, Susan. We've *never* had lunch together," she said.

"I know. You normally have lunch dates. Or when Alicia was still around, you met her quite often." Susan sat down. "You just look like you could use a friendly ear."

Peyton smiled. "Thank you. That's sweet of you." Ever since she'd cut Alicia out of her life—after Alicia's affair with Vicky—Peyton no longer had that one close friend she could talk to. She had friends, of course, but none that she could possibly share what was going on in her mind right now. Was it wise to share it with Susan, a woman who worked for her? Susan was a happily married woman with two kids. They had absolutely nothing in common other than work…and Susan's lesbian cousin, Jeannie. In the last year, yes, Susan had become a friend.

"I slept with her."

Susan's eyes widened only slightly. "I assume you mean Margot."

"Yes." Peyton buried her head in her hands. "It was awful."

"I'm sorry."

"Oh, God. I'm a horrible person." She looked at Susan. "Remember the woman that I met at the coast?"

"You mean the stranger you had sex with?"

Peyton rolled her eyes. "Yes, that one." She rested her elbows on her desk. "She was at the party."

Susan leaned back, surprise showing on her face. "Here? In Austin?"

Peyton nodded. "Seems she lives here. Small world, huh?"

"Oh, my God! Did she recognize you with your clothes on?"

"Of course she recognized me," Peyton snapped. Then, "Oh. You were teasing," she said as Susan's face broke out into a grin.

"Yes, I was teasing." She leaned forward again. "So she was at the party? What are the odds?"

"I know. The house that Margot had built, Logan's company did some custom painting or something." Peyton shook her head. "I couldn't believe it. I mean, I thought I'd never see her again. And I run into her at a party," she said with a laugh. Her smile faded quickly. "And then I slept with Margot."

"Well, it's been many years since I dated, but third date? I guess that's normal. Right? I mean, it's not like you just met her at the pool and then went off to her room or something."

"You really need practice with this friendly ear thing," Peyton said with a wave of her hand. "Sarcastic comments should be kept to yourself."

Susan laughed. "Sorry. So you slept with Margot. Go on," Susan encouraged.

"I didn't want to sleep with her."

"Then why did you?"

"Because of blonde Staci with the big breasts."

"Okay, I don't even pretend to understand lesbian dating, but you lost me with that one," Susan said.

"Staci was Logan's date. A pretty, young college student with enormous breasts," she explained. "Young. Really, really young. Like twenty-two. And really, really pretty." She sighed. "And I felt old and unattractive."

"And Margot made you feel young and pretty?"

"Yes. Only she wasn't the one I wanted to be with. And I wasn't...aroused," she said quietly, embarrassed to be discussing this with Susan. "And...so...I faked it."

Susan's laughter rang out. "You think you're the first woman to ever fake an orgasm?"

"You're missing the point. We slept together. She stayed the night. Do you have any idea how awkward it was the next morning?"

"She stayed the night?"

"Yes. And now that we've slept together, the next time she asks me out, she'll think it's a given that we'll have sex again." Peyton grabbed the bridge of her nose, not surprised by the headache that was starting.

"So don't go out with her again," Susan suggested.

"Then she'll think that the only reason I was dating her is because her name is Margot Joseph. And once we had sex, my mission was accomplished. Like that was all I wanted, which is so far from the truth."

Susan shook her head. "I don't follow your reasoning."

But Peyton's thoughts went elsewhere. She had been dreading Margot's call. In fact, she cringed every time her phone rang. Yet, it had been four days and she'd not heard from her. *Oh my God.* Maybe that was all Margot wanted. They had sex, so now she could move on to her next conquest.

"She hasn't called me."

Susan frowned.

"Margot. She hasn't called." Peyton smiled with relief. "Maybe she won't. Maybe all she wanted was to sleep with me. We did. So now she's going to, you know, move on."

"Well, if that makes you feel better, go with it." Susan stood. "So? We're good?"

Peyton laughed. "Yes. Thank you for being a friendly ear."

But her smile faded as soon as Susan left her office. She spun around in her chair, facing the window again, wondering how she was going to shake herself out of the doldrums she seemed to be in. Here she was, dating a woman ten years older than she was. And Logan was dating someone ten years younger. Why did that bother her so much? She should be happy with Margot. She was someone from her own circle. She fit in nicely with her friends. Peyton blew out her breath. Margot also didn't come close to rocking her world.

She leaned her head back and closed her eyes. Yes, doldrums, indeed. She needed a change.

She spun her chair around again, her gaze traveling over the dull, gray walls, the color matching her mood of late. She needed a change. Maybe some fresh paint—a bright color—would do the trick. A slow smile formed. She wondered if Weaver Painting Pros did offices. She wondered if she'd have the nerve to call them.

* * *

"Logan? I got a request for a bid."

Logan looked up from her computer, wondering why Mandy would mention this. They got requests for bids all the time. "And?"

"They asked for you. You want me to just send James out?"

"Yeah, that's fine," she said, going back to her spreadsheet. "Who was it?" she called after her.

Mandy walked back to her open door, looking at a piece of paper in her hand. "Watts and Associates, CPA. They're over on Balcones."

Logan shrugged. It didn't ring a bell. "Don't know them. Someone must have given him my name."

"It was a her. Peyton Watts," Mandy said.

Logan stared at her in surprise. "Peyton?"

"Yes. Ring a bell now?"

Logan grinned. Oh, yeah, bells were going off now. She held her hand out. "I'll do it." She stared at the information on the paper, hardly believing that Peyton had reached out to her.

Logan had all but convinced herself that meeting her at the party had been an aberration. "But do me a favor," she said. "Call her back. Schedule it for tomorrow, about eleven."

"Sure thing."

Logan saved the spreadsheet she'd been working on and closed up her laptop. She had shopping to do.

CHAPTER TWENTY-EIGHT

Peyton couldn't even begin to think about work as she stared at the clock, watching as it inched closer and closer to eleven. She couldn't believe how nervous she was. Would Logan even show up? The lady who had answered the phone told her that Logan didn't normally do bids.

She had actually come close to calling her back and canceling the whole thing. How silly was it that she had to go to these lengths just to see Logan? Why couldn't she have done something normal like call her up and ask her to lunch?

No, let's get the office painted instead.

Well, it was too late now. Seven more minutes. She stood, pacing slowly across her floor, pausing each time to glance out the window, then retracing her steps again. She knew it would be an enormous disappointment if Logan didn't show. But somehow, she knew she would. She literally jumped when her phone buzzed. She took a deep breath, then walked over, punching the intercom button.

"Yes, Susan."

"There's a…a painter here. Said you'd called for a bid?"

"Yes. I forgot to mention it to you," she lied. "I want to repaint all the offices."

"Shall I send her in?"

Her. Good.

"Yes, please."

Any nervousness she felt disappeared the moment Logan stepped into her office. Peyton covered her mouth to try to hide her smile, but she couldn't keep her laughter in. Logan was decked out, head to toe, in white, including a cute painter's hat. Logan's smiling eyes met hers, and they shared a quick laugh.

"As requested," Logan said with an exaggerated bow. "In case, you know, you have fantasies, I wanted you to see what I really looked like in painter's garb."

"Oh, my God. You look adorable," Peyton said, the words out before she could stop them.

"And for my fantasies, I now know what you look like in your fancy work outfit." Logan's gaze slid over her slowly. "However, I much prefer your bikini."

Peyton smiled broader. She just barely resisted closing her door and leaving them completely alone.

"How are you?"

"Great. Pretty surprised to get a request for a bid, though," Logan said. "Or did you just want to see me?"

"Both," Peyton said honestly as she sat, motioning for Logan to do the same. "We didn't really have much of a chance to visit the other night."

"No, we didn't. I still can't believe you were there." Logan's expression turned serious. "I didn't think I'd ever see you again."

"I know." She folded her hands together, smiling as Logan held her gaze. "So? You…you and…what was her name? Staci? Have you been dating long?"

"We've been out a few times," Logan said evasively. "And your third date with Margot Joseph? I trust you had a good time?"

Peyton felt herself blushing. "It was…okay," she said.

"Just okay?"

Peyton shook her head. "I'm not going to discuss Margot Joseph with you. Besides, I haven't spoken with her since then."

"No? That's odd. I haven't spoken with Staci since then either," Logan said with a quick smile. Logan rested her ankle across her knee, her gaze locked on Peyton's. "So, you really want to paint your office? Or do you want to get out of here, maybe grab some lunch?"

Peyton laughed. "In that outfit?"

Logan pulled at her white shirt. "I guess it's a little much, huh."

"But cute. And yes, I really want my office painted. We have four offices as well as the reception area and also a small break room."

Logan nodded. "Colors?"

"I don't have anything in mind. I'd like for each of my staff to pick out their own office color. Within reason, of course." She paused. "Do you normally do places like this?" she asked with a wave at her walls. "Or is it mostly homes?"

"Mostly homes, but not exclusively," Logan said. "We can do this for you." She grinned. "I'll give you a good price."

"I'd appreciate that," she said. She stood. "Let me show you around. Then maybe we can discuss lunch."

"Great. Let's get started."

But Peyton's phone rang before they could walk out, and she punched the intercom without thinking.

"Yes?"

"Margot Joseph is here," Susan said. "Send her in?"

Oh, God. Peyton's eyes flew to Logan, noting the disappointment she saw there.

"I'm sorry," she nearly whispered.

Logan shrugged. "No worries."

"Peyton?"

Peyton turned back to the phone. "Yes, Susan, send her in." She looked at Logan. "I don't—"

But she had no time to explain anything. Margot was there, walking into her office with a smile on her face. She stopped up short when she saw Logan.

"Oh. I didn't know you had someone," Margot said.

Peyton was at a loss for words. Thankfully, Logan was not. She immediately stuck her hand out.

"We met the other night at the party," Logan said. "Weaver Painting Pros. Just giving a bid."

"Of course. I thought you looked familiar," Margot said. She turned to Peyton. "I guess this is a bad time then. I was going to surprise you and steal you away for lunch."

"Well—"

"I can do the walkthrough without you," Logan offered. "Leave the bid with your secretary out there."

"Oh. Well—"

"Great," Margot said. "If we leave now, we can beat the lunch crowd. There's a little Italian place I've been dying to try."

Peyton looked helplessly at Logan, but Logan nodded.

"Sure. Go on. I'll be fine."

Their eyes met for a brief, intense moment. Peyton wanted so badly to tell Margot no, that she wouldn't have lunch with her. But then Logan looked away and Margot took her hand and she simply followed her out the door. Why must things be so complicated? How could a simple plan to get Logan to come over, to spend a little time with her—alone—go so wrong? She hadn't heard from Margot in five days. What were the odds that she'd pick that day to pop over and surprise her? Well, apparently, the odds were very good.

"I'm sorry I haven't called you," Margot said. "I've been swamped this week."

"It's okay," Peyton said. She glanced at Susan. "Lunch."

"Sure. What should I do with the painter?"

"Logan's going to give us a bid," she said. "Pick a color."

Susan's eyebrows shot up. "Logan?"

"Yes."

Peyton nodded slightly at Susan's unasked question. Yes, the same Logan who had charmed and flirted her way into Peyton's bed early that summer. Well, technically it had been Logan's bed, but only because they had been in a hurry and it had been closer. She smiled quickly as Susan shook her head slowly, as if scolding her.

Her smile faded, however, when Margot led her outside into the sunshine. It was hot and humid and her mood had soured.

Margot's sleek, black Mercedes waited and she held the door open for Peyton. She slid onto the leather seats with a heavy sigh, taking a glance back toward her office, wishing she was still inside...with Logan.

* * *

Logan pretended to be measuring the wall space when all she was doing was spying at the things in Peyton's office, trying to gain a little more insight into the woman. There didn't appear to be much here that was personal, she noted. She glanced over her shoulder, finding no one watching. She shouldn't be snooping, she knew, but she couldn't help herself. One more glance behind her, then she pulled the center drawer open on Peyton's desk. Something caught her attention as she was about to close it again.

A sand dollar.

It was placed carefully on a tissue, away from an assortment of pens and pencils. She reached out, touching it lightly, remembering the morning she'd given it to Peyton.

She kept it.

Logan slowly closed the drawer, feeling her chest tighten a bit. They'd watched the full moon, then had fallen asleep on the beach. The next morning, after the sunrise, she'd spotted the sand dollar as they were walking back. Over the years, Logan had found hundreds of them and no longer even looked for them anymore. But that morning, for some reason, she'd been drawn to it. And she'd handed it to Peyton, not knowing whether she cared for such things or not.

But she kept it. Maybe she wanted a reminder of her vacation. Logan slowly smiled.

And maybe she wanted a reminder of me.

"Excuse me."

Logan jumped and held a hand to her chest. She hoped she didn't have a guilty look on her face.

"I'm sorry, I didn't mean to startle you."

"No, it's okay. I was...I was mentally calculating the wall space, numbers running through my head," she said. "Peyton... Ms. Watts...said she wanted to paint all the offices."

"Yes, I've told the others. Would you like me to show you around?"

"Thank you, yes. You're Susan, right?"

"Right."

Logan bit her lip, wondering how much information Susan would be willing to share. She shouldn't be prying, but, oh well.

"So…Margot Joseph. She's nearly a celebrity, huh?"

"You think so?"

"Well, she's on TV," Logan said.

Susan snorted. "She's an ambulance chaser, as Peyton likes to say."

Logan laughed. "She said that?"

"You didn't hear it from me."

"And does she come over here often? You know, for lunch?"

Susan shook her head. "First time." Then she stopped. "Are you fishing for information?"

"Is it obvious?"

Susan looked her over, slowly nodding. "Maybe we should stick to painting. What do you say?"

Logan shrugged. "If we must."

CHAPTER TWENTY-NINE

"A blind date? Are you kidding me?"

Drew held her hands up. "It was Jay's idea, I swear."

Logan narrowed her eyes at her friend, trying to tell if she was lying or not. "Who is it?"

"You know her friend Audrey, right? Well, it's someone she works with. Kathy is her name."

Logan shook her head. "I don't want to go on a blind date. I can get my own dates, thank you very much."

"I told her you'd be pissed."

"What was she thinking?" Logan motioned to Rhonda at the bar, signaling for two beers.

"She was thinking that you've been moping around, that's what."

"I have not been moping around," Logan insisted. "I just haven't been in the mood to go out."

"Why don't you just call her up and ask her out?"

Logan didn't pretend not to know who Drew was talking about. They'd killed two bottles of wine the other night as she told them all about Peyton.

"Because she's dating Margot Joseph, that's why. I'm not exactly in her league," she said. "Besides, she's not my type."

"Here you are, ladies," Rhonda said, bringing them each a frosty mug of draft beer. "Will Jay be joining you?"

"Not if she knows what's best for her," Logan murmured.

Drew laughed. "Jay's coming later. We'll wait for her before ordering." When Rhonda left, Drew leaned closer. "Quit scowling," she teased. "So why is she not your type?"

"She's just not. And I'm certainly not hers. I think Margot Joseph…and women like her, that's her type."

"She called you," Drew reminded her.

"She wanted her office painted."

"Then why did she ask for you to give the bid?"

"Because she knows me." Logan shrugged. "Of course, she did say I looked cute in my painter's outfit."

Drew laughed. "I can't believe you did that. Did you take a picture?"

"No." Logan smiled. "I was kinda cute, though." Then she scowled again. "And then Margot shows up to take her to lunch. I haven't spoken to her since." She stared at Drew. "A blind date," she muttered. "Really?"

"Did I mention Kathy is forty-two?"

Logan spit her beer out. "That's older than you! My last date, she was twenty-two."

"Exactly."

"Your point?"

"Jay thought that since you were obviously infatuated with Peyton, who is older, that you needed to start dating more mature women."

"Older?" Logan shook her head. "First of all, I'm not infatuated with her. But I wouldn't really say she's older. It's only five years." Logan held her hand up to Drew. "Let's stop. I don't want to talk about Peyton. I *certainly* don't want to talk about a blind date."

Drew leaned forward. "Too late," she whispered, motioning behind Logan.

Logan turned her head slowly, seeing Jay smiling at her. Beside Jay stood a woman—a mature woman—dressed in a business suit. Logan slid her gaze back to Drew.

"I'm going to kill her."

* * *

After the impromptu lunch date with Margot, Peyton had managed to avoid dinner with her for the last week, coming up with an excuse both times Margot asked. She wasn't certain why she was avoiding her other than she didn't want another interrogation like she'd had at lunch. She felt like Margot had her on trial as she practically grilled her about her relationship with Logan. She tried to keep it as vague as possible, but she could tell Margot assumed they'd slept together. Frankly, she didn't care one way or the other.

But now here she was, sipping expensive wine, mingling with Margot's other guests as she hosted a party to show off her new home. Peyton knew quite a few of the guests—they were women from their circle. There was one in particular that she was curious about: Meredith Calhoun. Watching Meredith and Margot interact told her that they were more than friends. Whether that was a recent event or if they were old friends, Peyton didn't know. However, Margot never once attempted to hide it. That would have surprised her if not for the fact that Margot was paying her as much attention as she was Meredith. Which led her to believe that Margot was dating *both* of them.

How lovely.

She shouldn't have been surprised, though. Others had told her that Margot was a bit of a player. It really hadn't concerned her at the time, seeing as how she and Margot had no future whatsoever. But there were a few of her friends who gave her sympathetic looks whenever Margot and Meredith would chat. Of course, those same friends raised eyebrows whenever Margot came her way, making sure her wineglass was full and leaning in close to talk to her.

She realized then that that was Margot's game. As Logan had said, she was practically a celebrity. Well, not really, but Margot sure played the part. She was attractive. She was successful. And she could have anyone she wanted.

Peyton shook her head in disgust. *And I slept with her because I was jealous Logan was with Staci and her breasts.*

She wondered how rude it would be if she slipped away early, without an explanation, without a proper goodbye. She also wondered if she cared.

CHAPTER THIRTY

Logan drove slowly down the street, once again thinking that this was a *very* bad idea. She told herself that she wasn't going to be surprised if there was a car parked in Peyton's driveway. It would be Margot. She also told herself that she wouldn't be jealous. Peyton and Margot were dating. They were sleeping together. Disgusting to think about, sure, but it was what it was. But then as she crept nearer, another thought struck her.

She was a *stalker*.

She shook her head. Not really. No. She was just driving by. Nothing more. She didn't consider how she'd had to dig to get Peyton's address. Really, once she knew her name and her place of business, it wasn't all that hard. Really.

"God, you *are* a stalker," she murmured as she peered through the windshield, pleased that there wasn't a car parked in the driveway. Of course it was getting late. Maybe Peyton was already in bed. But no, there was a light on downstairs.

She drove past her house again, trying to convince herself that this was a really bad idea and to just go home. But as she circled around the block once more, she found herself pulling into Peyton's driveway. She feared if she made the block one more time, someone would call the cops.

Logan couldn't believe how nervous she was as she stood at the front door. She stared at the doorbell for the longest time, then finally reached out and pushed it. She heard the faint chime from inside. Minutes seemed to pass instead of seconds before she heard movement. Then the door opened and Peyton stood there, a surprised, yet questioning look on her face.

Logan grinned. "Good. You're up." She tapped her wrist as if wearing a watch. "We need to hurry."

"What? No," Peyton said, shaking her head. "I'm working."

"Working? It's too late to work," she said. "Come with me."

Peyton tilted her head. "Dare I ask where to?"

"Mount Bonnell," she said. "And we need to hurry."

"Mount Bonnell? No. Like you said, it's late. I have to go into the office tomorrow."

"Peyton, it's almost time. The midnight moon," she said.

A soft smile lit Peyton's face. "A full moon? Tonight?"

"Yeah, tonight." Logan motioned to her Jeep. "Come on. It'll be fun."

Peyton arched an eyebrow. "It's almost nine thirty."

"Yeah, well, we'll have to pretend it's midnight. Curfew. Park closes at ten."

Peyton took a deep breath, and Logan could see the indecision in her eyes. Logan gave what she hoped was a very charming smile. Apparently it was. Peyton finally nodded.

"Okay. I'll go with you to Mount Bonnell. At nine thirty. At night." She paused. "We're not going to get mugged, are we?"

Logan laughed. "What's with you and mugging? There'll just be people like us, watching the moon." She wiggled her eyebrows. "Some may be kissing and stuff like that, but we'll avoid them."

Peyton shook her head with a smile. "Why do I let you talk me into things like this?"

"Because I'm charming and irresistible," she said. "And you don't really want to be inside working, do you?" Then her eyes widened. "Unless you're not alone. Oh, God, you don't have company, do you?"

"Relax. I don't have company."

"Good. I thought maybe Margot was waiting for you in your bed or something."

Peyton rolled her eyes. "Would I really agree to go to Mount Bonnell with you if that was the case?"

Logan grinned. "Well, personally, that would be *my* choice."

Peyton just shook her head. She stepped back, motioning at herself. "Do I need to change?"

"No, no. You're perfect." She pointed at her bare feet. "Put some shoes on. Hiking boots if you have them."

"Yeah, right," Peyton murmured as she turned back inside her house.

Logan took that as an invitation to go inside herself, although she wasn't quite brazen enough to go snooping around. The house was nice. A little on the formal side, but nice. She followed the light and ended up in the doorway to what she assumed was Peyton's office.

"Being nosy?"

Logan turned around and shrugged. "Yeah."

"My office."

"I figured that," she said with a smile. "Ready?"

"Ready."

They drove in silence down MoPac, the traffic fairly light this evening. Logan glanced at Peyton several times, but Peyton kept her gaze straight ahead.

"You've been to Mount Bonnell before, right?"

Peyton shook her head. "No. Never."

"Really? I thought everyone goes at least once," she said. "Nice views. It overlooks the river...Lake Austin and the million dollar homes that line it," she added.

Peyton finally turned to her. "The other day...I'm sorry that Margot showed up. I had no idea."

"It's okay," Logan said. "You got my bid?"

"Yes. I accept."

"Great. I'll get a team out there."

"Will you come?"

Logan put her blinker on and exited off MoPac, slowing as she came to the light. "They really don't like to let me paint," she said with a quick laugh. "But I guess I could supervise."

She took 35th Street to Mount Bonnell Road and drove slowly up the hill. She was surprised to find quite a few cars still there. They wouldn't have much time before curfew but enough to get to the top.

Peyton stood at the base, staring at the endless steps that went straight up. She turned to Logan. "Really?"

Logan ginned. "One hundred steps." Then she laughed. "But let's go around to the side and hike up. Not quite as strenuous."

The lights in the parking area chased some of the shadows away, but she was prepared. She pulled a small flashlight from her back pocket, then took Peyton's hand.

"Don't want you to trip on a rock," she said. She was pleased that Peyton didn't pull away.

They didn't speak as they hiked up the trail. They heard voices occasionally as other people had pulled off the trail onto overlooks…or to steal a kiss or two. When they got to the top, there were three other couples there, two were looking out over the river, the other one was reading the historical marker. Logan led them away to the other side. She turned a circle, finding the moon. It wasn't yet high overhead, but it was still quite impressive as it hovered over the city.

"Ten minutes until curfew," she said quietly. "It's beautiful, isn't it?"

Peyton stared at the moon for a long moment, then turned to her. Their eyes held and Peyton squeezed her hand.

"Very."

Logan nodded. "Yeah. Very."

She was fairly certain they were no longer talking about the moon. But then Peyton dropped her hand and turned back to it and the moment passed. After a few minutes, Logan tugged her over to the edge, pointing out the river—and Lake Austin—below them.

"The 360 Bridge is over there. Pennybacker Bridge," she said. "It's got a great overlook too." She turned to Peyton. "Maybe I'll take you sometime."

Peyton smiled. "That would be nice."

Logan looked away for a second, then back. "Listen, you and Margot, is that like…really serious?"

Peyton shook her head. "I found out she wanted me to be one in a small harem of women she dated. That's not my thing." She turned her gaze back to the river. "Besides, I'm not...really attracted to her."

"No?" Logan tried to keep the smile off her face and thought she did a pretty good job of it. "Well, I was thinking. Down at the coast, we didn't exactly get to know each other, seeing as how we didn't even share last names or where we lived," she said.

Peyton laughed. "I thought you were a stalker."

"Oh, I am," Logan said with a smile. "I found your house, didn't I?"

"True."

"Anyway, I thought maybe we could...go out. You know, do things together. No hanky-panky," she said quickly. "Just...get to know each other."

Peyton held her stare. "Like a platonic relationship?"

Logan leaned closer. "Honey, I can assure you, platonic is not in my vocabulary when it comes to you." She cleared her throat and smiled. "I just thought, you know, since I'm not your type and you're not my type...maybe we don't know enough about each other to really say we're not the right type."

Peyton nodded. "Okay. But what about...Staci? Will she mind if we go out and do things together?"

"Actually, I haven't seen Staci since that night at the party." She wasn't sure how much to tell Peyton, but she decided she wouldn't lie. "She wanted to have sex and I wasn't really in the mood." She held Peyton's gaze in the moonlight. "Not with her, anyway," she added quietly. She was surprised by the sad look she saw in Peyton's eyes. She would have thought that she'd have been happy.

"I...I slept with Margot that night," Peyton said. "Mainly because...because I saw you there with Staci and I...I—"

But Peyton turned away and said no more, instead looking back toward the city, her back to Logan. *Damn.* She wasn't really ready for the stab of jealousy she felt. Logan was about to reach for her, but she heard the call from down below of curfew and knew they had to leave. Peyton must have heard it too, because she turned again but avoided looking at Logan. Logan wasn't sure what Peyton expected her to say. She flipped the flashlight back on and waited. Peyton shook her head, though, indicating she didn't want to talk. Instead, they were silent on the way down.

Back in the Jeep, they sat quietly, neither speaking. When Logan went to start it, however, Peyton stopped her with a light touch on her arm.

"Thank you for coming by the house tonight," she said. "Since the other day at the office, I've wanted to call you, but I really didn't know what to say."

"It doesn't have to be this hard, Peyton."

Peyton looked away. "I feel like my world is all messed up."

Logan took her hand and folded it between her own. "Messed up? Why?"

"Nothing seems...*right* anymore," Peyton said. "I'm surrounded by people I know, doing things I've always done, yet I feel so...so lonely."

Logan stared into her eyes, wondering what she was trying to say.

"Even now?" she asked quietly.

Peyton gave her a half smile. "No. Not now. That's why everything feels all messed up. I hardly know you, yet..." she said, her voice trailing off.

"Well, you'll get to know me." She loosened her grip on Peyton's hand, bringing it to her lips for a light kiss. "And just so you know, I kinda feel a little messed up too. I mean, I've turned into a stalker," she said with a laugh, trying to lighten the mood. "I circled your block three times before I got the nerve to go up to your house."

Peyton gave her a sweet smile. "I'm glad you stopped. A new adventure. Mount Bonnell."

"And another full moon to add to your list."

"It was pretty. But I think I liked it better down at the coast."

Logan gave her a flirty grin. "I liked a *lot* of things better down at the coast."

CHAPTER THIRTY-ONE

Peyton stood back in horror as Logan helped shove her office furniture to the middle of the room. She wasn't sure what she expected, but Logan was in shorts and a T-shirt, like the rest of her crew. While they were all in shoes, Logan wore the sandals that Peyton remembered from the coast. She stepped back as one of the guys flung out a plastic cover and tossed it over her furniture.

"It'll be back in place tomorrow," Logan promised. "Now you have to leave. I'm the only supervisor allowed on this project."

"Okay. But I'll be right out there if you need me."

"Oh, I'll need you, I'm certain of that," Logan said, flashing her the flirty smile that Peyton loved.

Peyton returned her smile, then went out to sit in the reception area. It had been five days since their Mount Bonnell adventure and the weekend had come and gone. It was a long, lonely weekend; she kept hoping Logan would show up. She made a mental note to give Logan her phone number. Friends did that, right?

She had replayed their conversation from that night over and over. Logan wanted to get to know her. No hanky-panky. Staci was apparently out of the picture. And God, surely Margot was as well. Peyton had only gotten an email from her, saying she was sorry she didn't get to spend much time with her at her house party. Apparently Margot didn't know that Peyton had intentionally slipped away early without seeking her out. It didn't matter. Even if Margot called and asked her to dinner, Peyton would decline. She now knew enough about Margot to realize she wasn't even someone she wanted to be friends with, let alone date.

But did she want to date Logan? Is that what they'd be doing? Getting to know each other by dating? Did no hanky-panky mean no kissing too? Peyton felt her face flush. Yes, it must. Because if they kissed, it would definitely lead to more. Just being around Logan, looking into her smiling eyes, feeling her positive energy, Peyton felt the pull of her attraction. Being near Logan made everything feel bright and fresh...and new. And if Logan wanted to skip the "getting to know you" part and jump back into a sexual relationship, Peyton wouldn't protest. But was that all she wanted out of this? Just a sexual relationship?

"Do you plan to sit out here all day?"

Peyton blinked her thoughts away as she looked at Susan. "Will it bother you?"

"Would it bother you if I sat in one of your visitor's chairs all day while you tried to work?"

"Yes. But I'm the boss," Peyton reminded her. "Besides, you're not that busy. September is the best time to do this."

"No. November would have been the best time."

"I didn't want to wait until November."

"Are you ready to talk about it yet?"

"I assume you mean Logan," she said.

"Well, that and your sudden out-of-the-blue urge to get the office painted," Susan said.

"I felt like a change."

"In your office or in your life?"

Peyton smiled. "Both." She leaned forward, lowering her voice. "She's attractive, isn't she?"

"Yes, she is. And, well, I kinda like her," Susan said. "Not at all what I imagined your vacation lover to be like."

Peyton felt herself blushing, but she laughed. "And what were you imagining?"

"Well, you said she was young and not your type, so I pictured a young skanky woman with multiple tattoos, perhaps a piercing or two."

"Oh my God!"

"But Logan seems normal. And cute. I like her for you much more than Margot Joseph. I don't know why you say she's not your type."

"I know. I'm not sure what my type is anymore," she said. She met Susan's eyes and smiled. "We're going to…get to know each other better."

"Oh? Like date?"

"I'm not sure. I think Logan's idea of dating might be completely different than mine. I can't see us going to fancy restaurants."

"Or lectures?"

Peyton laughed. "Especially that. But…I like her. She makes me feel good. Inside and out."

Susan nodded. "We should all try to add people to our lives who make us happy. And I will say you do seem to be smiling a lot more lately."

"Yes. Plus, Margot hasn't called. I hope that's over with." She stood, walking to the window. "Do you think I should invite her to lunch?"

"Margot?"

Peyton spun around. "No. Not Margot," she said. "Logan."

"Well, if you're going to get to know each other better, that's a good way to start," Susan said. "Of course, you're in your suit and she's in shorts. Going to be hard to find common ground."

Peyton glanced at her suit and sighed. Her first job out of college had been for a large accounting firm. They had a strict dress code. Business suits only. Casual Fridays were only a slightly less toned down version of the business suit. When she bought this firm, she'd kept the habit, insisting that her staff do the same. But they were a small firm with mostly individual clients.

Over the years, the others had adopted a more casual wardrobe, especially on Fridays. Yet she still maintained her staunch practice of dressing in conservative business suits, even during the brutal summer months.

She knew she dressed the part because it was the image she'd created for herself. But it also fit in with most of her friends, professional women like herself. Margot, for instance, wouldn't dare be caught out in public in anything other than a business suit. The few times they'd been out to dinner together, they'd each been dressed as if they were heading to an important board meeting.

She turned back to the window, her gaze on the street outside, remembering when Logan had first come to her office. She'd commented on her "fancy work outfit," saying she preferred the bikini instead. She smiled as she pictured them back at the coast, both of them in their bikinis. She had taken Logan's words at face value, but was there an underlying meaning? Was she saying she preferred the more casual Peyton she'd met at the coast? Peyton stepped back, again looking at her dull gray business suit, her black pumps. Was she comfortable? Of course not. It was hot and her feet hurt.

"You're frowning."

Peyton spun around, finding Logan watching her. Logan, in her shorts and sandals, who looked completely comfortable and at ease. She had a questioning look on her face, but Peyton shook her head.

"Just thinking."

Logan motioned with her head back to Peyton's office. "Want to come take a look? Make sure you like it before we proceed."

"Yes, okay."

The color Peyton had picked out was a conservative cream, just enough of a change from the original drab gray. She shook her head. It was now just a dull, drab cream.

"I hate it." She turned to Logan. "I need a change."

Logan arched an eyebrow.

"I need a...a *color*. Something *fun*," she said.

Logan nodded. "Okay. The other offices, they all picked out some brighter colors. Two of them wanted an accent wall. Why don't we paint those first?" she suggested. "Maybe you'd like something like that."

Peyton stared at her bare walls. "Yes." She glanced at Logan. "I'm sorry."

"No, no. I want you to be satisfied," she said. Then that flirty grin appeared. "In everything," she added.

Peyton laughed and nodded. "Yes, thank you."

"So, I guess you want your office back, huh?"

"Just enough so I can get a little work done," she said.

"Okay. Scoot," Logan said, waving her out of the room.

At the door, Peyton turned back to her.

"Logan? Lunch?"

Logan nodded. "Sure. Order pizza."

* * *

"Can you at least take your shoes off? I feel terribly underdressed."

Peyton tugged at the collar of her blouse. "We're sitting on the patio, it's in the nineties and I'm in a business suit. I feel terribly *over*dressed," Peyton said.

"We could have eaten inside with everyone else," Logan offered.

"I know. But…I wanted some alone time," Peyton admitted.

"So relax then. Take your shoes off."

Peyton shook her head. "I can't. My toenails aren't polished."

"So? If I recall, they weren't polished down at the coast either," she said.

"Honestly, I don't really like my nails polished. And I was on vacation. I also rarely put makeup on while I was there either," Peyton said.

Logan put her slice of pizza down. "Peyton, it's just me here. I don't know what the rules are, but I kinda like your feet and toes the way they were." She held her foot up. "You know, mine aren't painted either."

Peyton laughed. "I can't picture you getting a pedicure."

"I actually like pedicures," she said. "I just don't let them get near me with nail polish." She picked up her pizza again. "So, did you have a good weekend?"

Peyton shrugged. "It was…a break. I didn't do anything. Stayed by the pool most of the time."

"Oh? You go skinny-dipping?"

Peyton laughed. "No, I did not."

"You like to swim?"

"My lone form of exercise," Peyton said as she finally kicked off her shoes. "Oh, yes, that feels better."

Logan smiled but didn't say anything. She took a big drink from her tea but couldn't help but glance at Peyton's bare feet. She had a quick flash as she remembered those feet rubbing against her calf as they were making love. She shook the image away.

"Are you free on Saturday?"

Peyton bit into her pizza, eyebrows raised.

"You want to go to the lake?" Logan asked. "Ted—my dad—he's got a small weekend place there. He's got a boat. My friends Drew and Jay are going out with me." She took another slice of pizza from the box. "You met Jay at that party," she said.

Peyton nodded. "Yes, I remember her."

"So? Interested?"

Peyton met her gaze and smiled. "Yes. Interested."

"Great." She let out a relieved sigh. She'd been afraid Peyton would decline. Or worse, she feared she already had plans…with Margot. "I'll pick you up. We'll go by Drew's place first. You'll love their house. Especially their pool. I can't wait to show it to you. It's spring-fed."

"Really?"

"Yeah, you'll love it."

Peyton picked up her phone. "Maybe we should, you know, exchange phone numbers."

Logan laughed. "Do you often give your number to stalkers?"

"No. You'll be the first."

CHAPTER THIRTY-TWO

Logan held the back gate open to Drew's garden and pool, letting Peyton go in first.

"You'll love them. They're super nice," she said.

"Will you quit worrying that I won't like them?" Peyton said.

"I know. It's just…they're my best friends." And it was important that Peyton like them.

Peyton stopped. "I'm happy to be here with you, Logan. And I'm looking forward to spending time with them. I'm sure I'll like them just fine."

"Well, they're probably not like…well, not like your friends," she said.

Peyton took her hand, smiling slightly. "Good. Then it'll be a pleasant change."

"Okay, then. I'll quit worrying."

Drew and Jay were sitting on the patio, the ceiling fan turning overhead. After their work during the summer on remodeling the pool house and outdoor kitchen, whenever Logan came over, they rarely used the house at all. They stood when Logan and Peyton approached. Drew held her hand out.

"You must be Peyton," she said. "I'm Drew Montgomery. Welcome."

"Thanks. Nice to meet you," Peyton said.

"You remember Jay," Logan said.

"Yes. Good to see you again."

"Glad you came, Peyton," Jay said. "Would you like something to drink?"

"Beer? Wine cooler? Water?" Drew offered.

"I'll have a beer," Logan said.

"That's fine with me," Peyton said.

"Good. I'll show you around the pool," Jay said. "Drew and Logan can get the drinks."

Logan followed Drew into the opened kitchen. She took a beer from the fridge and handed Drew a wine cooler.

"No. I'll have a beer with you," Drew said.

"Giving up wine coolers finally?"

"I like fruity drinks, what can I say." Drew tipped her bottle in Logan's direction in a silent toast before drinking. "She's cute."

"Yeah, she is," Logan said. "I'm nervous."

"You? Why?"

"Because this is kinda like, you know, a date."

Drew laughed. "And you're used to twenty-something college students?"

Logan shrugged. "I like her. A lot."

Drew's expression turned serious. "Like…she's the one?"

Logan nodded. "I could fall in love with her."

Drew surprised her by pulling her into a quick hug. "Good for you."

Logan laughed. "God, don't let Jay catch us hugging. We'll never hear the end of it."

"Too late," Jay said behind them. "What did we miss?"

"Nothing," Logan said. "Girl talk."

Jay laughed. "You two? Girl talk? That's a first." She turned to Peyton. "And this is the outdoor kitchen. Logan helped with all the remodeling. In fact, she was here most weekends this summer."

"It's fabulous," Peyton said. "It's so inviting. And I'm very jealous of your pool."

"Feel free to take a swim," Drew offered. "I'm assuming you have your suit on under your shorts."

"Or it's clothing optional," Logan added with a wink at Peyton.

"With you around, I don't doubt it," Peyton said with a smile.

"Oh, Drew too," Jay said. "She loves skinny-dipping. I've caught these two playing like teenagers in here before."

"Now don't start telling her our secrets," Logan said. "She might get the wrong impression."

Logan smiled contentedly as Peyton was absorbed into their little group with ease. The four of them sat around the patio table, chatting like old friends. She didn't know why she was so worried that Peyton wouldn't fit in or that Peyton wouldn't like Drew and Jay. She seemed very comfortable, and she contributed to the conversation as much as anyone. Logan thought it couldn't have gone better. That is, until Jay mentioned the blind date.

"You should have seen Logan's eyes," Jay said with a laugh. "I thought she was going to kill me."

"Don't think I wasn't planning on it," she said.

"So how many times did you go out with her?" Peyton asked, an innocent smile on her face.

"Are you kidding me? She was forty-two and acted fifty-two," Logan said. "She has three kids. She talked about them and her divorce most of the night. I couldn't wait to get out of there."

"I'm sorry," Jay said. "I don't know what I was thinking. Audrey swore she was over her husband." Jay turned to Peyton. "Audrey's my best friend. I told her I was looking for someone a little more mature than college age."

"Okay." Logan stood up quickly. "I think we've about covered everything. Let's go to the lake." The other three laughed at her attempt to end the conversation, and she shrugged with a smile.

"No more blind date talk, huh?" Peyton asked.

"Nope. I'm ready to hit the water."

* * *

Peyton laughed delightfully as Logan attempted to show off on skis. However, her second attempt at a flip failed miserably and she crashed into the lake. Drew killed the throttle on the boat and turned around, circling Logan as she bobbed in the water.

"Very nice," Peyton said.

Logan grinned. "You ready to try it?"

Peyton shook her head. "I can't ski."

"Have you tried?"

"No. That's why I know I can't."

"Well, I'll have to teach you sometime," she said. "Drew? Ready?"

"Yep."

Drew helped Logan back into the boat, then she jumped overboard. She floated on her back as she put the skis on. Logan toweled off, leaving her hair a tousled mess. But it was an adorable tousled mess, Peyton noted. She turned back to Jay, not wanting to blatantly stare at Logan in her bikini. She knew every inch of her body, and the bikini did little to hide her most favorite parts.

"I saw you looking," Logan said with her usual flirty smile.

Peyton grinned back at her. "There's really no need for me to look. I've already seen it all."

Jay laughed loudly. "Oh, Logan. I think you've met your match here."

"Don't encourage her," Logan said as she got behind the wheel.

Jay leaned closer to her. "I'm so glad you came today. It's such a nice change."

"From her usual dates?"

Jay nodded. "We love Logan to death. I so want her to be happy." She glanced quickly at Logan, who was watching Drew. "I don't want to presume more than what it is, but it seems almost like fate that you two ran into each other again at our party."

Peyton looked at Logan too. Was it fate? Then Logan turned and their eyes met. It caused Peyton's breath to catch. Only Drew giving the go-ahead from the water broke their stare. Logan turned away, putting the boat in motion, and Peyton turned her attention to Drew as she, like Logan, got up effortlessly on the skis.

The afternoon seemed to fly by as they alternated between skiing, swimming and playing in the water and just cruising around the lake in the boat. She and Logan had teased, flirted and played until she was laughing with delight. She couldn't remember the last time she'd had such a carefree day of play. She smiled as, yes, she *could* remember. It was down at the coast with Logan.

But now, after a sunset dinner at a small barbeque place and goodbye hugs with Drew and Jay, Logan was taking her back home, signaling an end to the fun-filled day.

"You tired?" Logan asked.

"I am," she said as she lazily rolled her head Logan's way. "I had a wonderful time, Logan. Thank you for inviting me."

"I had a great time too," Logan said. She glanced at her quickly. "So, you liked Drew and Jay, right?"

"Oh, I loved them," she said. "In fact, Jay and I exchanged phone numbers."

"You did? Good."

"It was a really fun day."

"Yeah, it was. But September is nearly gone. Might be the last time out on the lake. At least, in the water," Logan said. She reached across the console and found Peyton's hand. Peyton's fingers entwined with hers, resting their clasped hands on her thigh. It felt nice.

"So that was your father's place? Does he go there often?"

"Practically every weekend during the summer. But he lets me have the boat if I want. He just likes to sit, fish and drink beer," she said.

Peyton turned in her seat, facing Logan. "You never said where you lived."

"No? Well, it's not too far from Drew's place, really. I live in a duplex," Logan said.

"Really? I wouldn't have guessed that," she said. "What if you hate your neighbor?"

Logan grinned. "Then I kick them out."

"Oh. You *own* the duplex."

"Yeah. There are four there. My dad built two and I built two," Logan said. "I never really intended on living there. I was going to buy a house somewhere. But everything I looked at just wasn't me. I think I'm trying to find a place like Drew's, and that will never happen."

"Yes, that was unique. Her grandfather had great vision."

"Yeah. And they don't mind me popping over all the time. But I try not to overstay my welcome," Logan said. "Then again, if I miss a few days, Jay calls and thinks something's wrong."

Logan slowed as she turned onto Peyton's street and Peyton sighed, knowing their time together was coming to an end. Logan pulled into her driveway but left the Jeep running. Their hands were still touching, and Peyton squeezed Logan's lightly, relishing the contact. They hadn't spent a moment alone all day, but that didn't mean they hadn't shared any intimate moments. They had. Even at dinner, they'd sat close to each other in the small booth, their thighs brushing, their hands touching, their eyes meeting. She had hoped that their no "hanky-panky" rule would be broken, but apparently not. Logan finally pulled her hand away. Peyton missed the contact immediately.

"It…it was a great day," Peyton said again.

"The best."

"Yes." She paused. "Well, I guess I should go in."

Logan nodded. "Yes. You should." Their eyes met. "And you should hurry," she added in a whisper. Peyton's tongue came out to wet her dry lips, and Logan's gaze followed. "Peyton, please… you should go."

She didn't want to go. At least, not alone. She wanted to drag Logan inside with her. But she was only torturing herself—and Logan—by staying. Amazing how she could be so aroused by this woman and they had barely touched. She finally moved, taking off her seat belt at least. But instead of getting out, she leaned across the console, kissing Logan gently on her cheek. Logan didn't pull away and Peyton's mouth lingered, brushing the corner of Logan's mouth. She heard Logan's quick intake of breath, felt her own pulse spring to life.

"Do you have any idea how badly I want to make love to you?" Logan whispered.

Peyton closed her eyes. "Absolutely," she murmured. All she had to do was turn a fraction and their mouths would meet. A kiss would be their undoing. But this wasn't about sex, she reminded herself. This was about getting to know each other better *without* sex. She nearly growled as she pulled away. "*God*…Logan."

Logan nodded. "I know." She gave a quick smile. "Cold shower. That's what I'm going to do."

Peyton laughed and opened the door. She grabbed the bag she'd brought along for her change of clothes, then stood beside the Jeep.

"Be careful, please."

"For sure. I'll see you later."

Peyton watched her drive away, not going inside until the Jeep's taillights faded from sight. Yes, cold shower indeed.

CHAPTER THIRTY-THREE

Peyton leaned back in her office chair, her phone held casually to her ear. She was smiling uncontrollably as Logan told her about the paint mishap from that morning. Her laughter was music to her ears.

"It could have been on the *Three Stooges*," Logan said. "It was only a four-foot ladder, thankfully, but it was two gallons of paint on my head. I really need to stick with supervising."

"Surely someone got a picture?" Peyton asked.

"Unfortunately, yes. I'm sure it's all over Facebook by now," Logan said with a laugh. "I'll be sure to send it to you."

"It's a shame that didn't happen when you were finishing up here. I could have seen it firsthand," she said.

They were quiet for a moment, then Logan cleared her throat. "I should probably let you get back to work."

Peyton glanced at her laptop, knowing she had several accounts that needed her attention. None were as appealing as chatting with Logan, however.

"I have a few minutes," she said.

"Yeah? Long enough for me to talk dirty to you?"

"That depends on what kind of dirty," she said, smiling. "Will I need to close my door?"

"That could be fun. Phone sex."

"Doesn't that fall into the no hanky-panky rule?"

"I suppose. Whose rule was that, anyway?"

Peyton laughed. "That would be you."

"Yeah. What was I thinking?"

Peyton's smiled faded. "Are you ready to break it?"

"Do you want to make love with me?"

Peyton felt her face flush, her heartbeat increase. She took a quick breath. "Yes."

Logan paused, but Peyton could hear her subtle breathing. "We haven't really, you know, dated much."

"We spent an entire day together. That takes the place of several two- and three-hour dates," she countered.

"Yeah. We could say that, couldn't we?"

Peyton heard the smile in her voice, and she smiled too. "Gets my vote."

Logan laughed. "You're too easy."

She heard Susan clear her throat behind her and Peyton spun around guiltily, wondering how long she'd been standing there listening. *Damn.*

"Umm, I need to go," she said.

"Everything okay?"

"Yes. Susan is standing here tapping her foot, though. I think she needs me."

"I see. Okay then. Talk to you later."

"Bye."

She put her phone down, then looked expectantly at Susan. Susan simply smiled at her and shook her head.

"What?"

"Your laughter was interrupting the office."

"It was not." But she smiled. "She makes me laugh."

"Yes. And I've never quite seen you like this before. Are you in love with her?"

Peyton nearly gasped. "In love? We hardly know each other. How could I possibly be in love with her?"

"Peyton, I was here when you met Vicky, when you dated her. When you slept with her, I was here. When she moved into your home, I was here. And never once did I ever see you like this."

"Like what?"

"Smiling. Happy."

"It was…it was different with Vicky, yes." She leaned back in her chair. "Logan is so unlike Vicky. She's unlike anyone I've ever dated before." And she had to admit, Logan would be so easy to fall in love with. If she dared.

* * *

Logan hung up the phone with only one thing on her mind. Seeing Peyton. After the weekend's trip to the lake, she thought she'd give Peyton some time. Time for what, she wasn't sure. They'd talked on the phone each day, but now, Wednesday, she was ready to see her. She hoped Peyton was as well.

She thought maybe they could have lunch outdoors. While the expected cool front hadn't hit yet, there was very little humidity, giving the day a fallish feel even though the temperature was approaching ninety.

Logan felt her anticipation build as she turned the corner. She spotted Peyton's office building and slowed, parking her Jeep behind a black Mercedes that had just pulled up. She turned the engine off, shocked to find Margot Joseph getting out.

Damn.

Well, she wasn't going to hide in the Jeep. She got out as well, and when she slammed her door, Margot turned in her direction. Logan flashed her a smile.

"Dang, you beat me here by a minute."

Margot didn't appear amused. "I beat you by far more than a minute. And unless you have some painting to do, you should just run along."

Logan was shocked by her tone…and her words. They actually left her speechless. Apparently Margot wasn't through.

"You can't compete with me."

Logan regained some of her composure. She gave Margot an uninterested shrug. "Oh? I wasn't aware there was a competition."

Margot's smile was piercing. "Which is precisely why you're going to lose." She looked Logan over with disgust. "That's how you dress when you're trying to impress Peyton?"

Logan looked down at her shorts and sandals. She wiggled her toes and nodded. "Yeah. It's nearly ninety degrees." It was her turn to measure Margot. "You're in a suit and…pantyhose? Really? Do women still wear pantyhose?" She shook her head. "Anyway, I'd say I'm a lot more comfortable than you are."

Margot's smile was condescending. "What does comfort have to do with it? It's an image. Of course, at your age, you probably don't have a clue, do you?" Her smile turned into a smirk. "As I said, you can't compete with me. I always win." She took a step toward the office, then stopped. "Goodbye," she said pointedly.

Logan stood there as Margot marched up the sidewalk and to the office door. She blew out her breath and turned, going back to her Jeep. She thought she'd just drive around the block a few times and wait for Peyton to get rid of her.

Exactly six minutes later, she parked again at Peyton's office, thankful the black Mercedes was gone. The encounter with Margot had zapped some of her good humor, but now the prospect of lunch with Peyton brought it back. She was actually whistling as she walked up to the door.

Susan looked at her with surprise as she went inside. Logan nodded at her, then motioned toward Peyton's office.

"The boss in?"

"No. She just left for lunch."

Logan felt her heart fall to her feet. *Damn.* "Oh. I see." She paused. "With Margot?"

Susan nodded. "Yes. It wasn't a planned date, if that's what you're thinking. Margot just showed up. She does that sometimes."

"Yeah, I know. I actually saw her when she got here. I thought, well, that Peyton would decline, that's all." She gave a quick smile. "I was kinda going to ask her out to lunch myself. Guess I should have come earlier, huh."

"Maybe you should have just called and asked," Susan suggested.

"Yeah. I suppose." She shrugged again, feeling totally dejected. "Well, it's none of my business anyway." She took a step back. "I guess I'm going to get out of here." She nodded at her. "Good to see you again."

She nearly ran back to her Jeep, totally embarrassed by the jealousy she felt. Did she really think that Peyton would turn down a lunch date with Margot Joseph? Maybe Margot was right; she couldn't compete with her. She sat in her Jeep, looking down at herself. Shorts and sandals? Yeah, she felt young and childish. Margot was mature. She was sophisticated. She didn't do stupid things like haul Peyton up to Mount Bonnell at night to catch the moon. No, Margot most likely took her to fancy and expensive restaurants.

Damn.

CHAPTER THIRTY-FOUR

Peyton sipped from the crystal glass, surprised that Margot ordered wine for their lunch. Actually, she was surprised that Margot had showed up at all. She'd not spoken to her since her party.

"So, I must ask," Margot said. "Are you avoiding me?"

"Avoiding you? No. You haven't called."

"Well, you just disappeared the other night at my house. I thought maybe...something upset you."

Peyton nodded, deciding to be honest with Margot. "Actually, it was a bit uncomfortable that evening. You made it quite obvious to everyone there that you were dating Meredith Calhoun."

"I am. Or rather, I was." Margot flashed a quick smile. "I rarely date exclusively. I thought you knew that."

"Yes, I do." Peyton paused, trying to find a tactful way to say what she was thinking. "And while I enjoy your company, I don't really see a future for us, Margot. Nothing more than friends, anyway. I don't know that I want to be one of a handful of women you date."

"Is that any different than me being a handful of women *you* date?"

Peyton was taken aback by the question. "I don't know what you mean?"

"The painter. What's her name? Logan Weaver?"

Peyton was shocked Margot would bring up Logan. "What about her?"

"You obviously have some sort of relationship with her. I could tell that when you ran into her at that party." Margot's smile was a little condescending. "She's really not your type, though, is she? I mean, she's a painter."

"And that's a less noble profession than, say, suing insurance companies?"

Margot seemed shocked by her words, but then she laughed. "Good one, Peyton."

Peyton nodded. "And you're right, Logan doesn't appear to be my type. But she's…fun. Different."

"So you *are* dating then?"

Peyton tilted her head, pondering what to call it. "We've gone out. I'm not sure I'd exactly call it dating," she said vaguely.

"I guess not, seeing as how she was dressed today."

Peyton frowned. "Today? What do you mean?"

"Oh, I beat her to your office by a few seconds," Margot laughed. "She wasn't exactly dressed for lunch, but I'm sure that was her intention." Margot picked up her wineglass. "We had a…a nice little discussion."

Oh, God, Logan had come by her office? Peyton could only imagine the discussion Margot had with her. And no, Logan probably wasn't dressed for lunch *here*, but she would have still been perfect. And suddenly she wanted nothing more than for the lunch to be over with. She shouldn't have accepted the invitation in the first place, but she couldn't think of an excuse to decline and she hadn't wanted to be rude. Now she wished she had been.

"I don't give up, you know."

Peyton brought her thoughts back to Margot. "Excuse me?"

"I never give up the pursuit, Peyton."

Peyton met her gaze. "I wasn't aware that I was prey."

* * *

Peyton gave Margot a hurried "thanks for lunch" as she got out of her car. The lunch had been endless and their conversation had been strained. To top it off, she had to confirm a date with Margot to the annual banquet for her local CPA professional organization. She was running for president this year, and, at the time, Margot had seemed like the perfect date. She was well respected in the business community and also well known. Even then, Peyton had still almost canceled. Almost. But she vowed it would be the last time she went out with Margot. *Prey*, my ass, she thought as she walked into the office. She went immediately to Susan.

"Logan? Did she come in?"

Susan smiled. "And yes, how was your lunch?"

Peyton shook her head. "Awful. Margot said she ran into Logan here. I guess she left. I didn't see her Jeep," she said.

"Yes, she came by."

"Did you tell her I went to lunch with Margot?"

"I didn't have to tell her. Like you said, she saw Margot. From what I gather, Logan left, thinking you would decline Margot's invitation. She was planning to come back after Margot was gone." Susan shrugged. "I told her she should have just called you and asked you to lunch herself."

"Was she…upset?"

"Upset? Well, she was something. I'm not sure upset is the word I'd use."

Peyton threw her hands up. "How can it possibly be this complicated? I don't even like Margot. In fact, she is a pompous ass. I don't think I saw that before."

"How could you not? She is as pretentious as they come," Susan said.

"Oh, God, I know. And now I've got that banquet to go to with her." She headed to her office, then stopped. "So did Logan say anything? I mean, for you to give me a message or anything?"

"No. All she said was that it was none of her business, and she was just going to get out of here."

"What does that mean?"

"None of her business that you were out with Margot, I guess."

"I wasn't *out* with Margot," she muttered as she slammed her office door. She took her phone out of her purse, calling Logan. After the fourth ring, she knew it would go unanswered. When Logan's voice mail came on, she was lost as to what to say. She disconnected without speaking.

"Oh, Logan…please don't disappear on me."

CHAPTER THIRTY-FIVE

Logan towel-dried her hair, then looked into the mirror, making sure she'd gotten all the paint off her face. It's no wonder the guys didn't want her helping them. She ended up with more on her than on the walls. She took her time getting dressed, knowing no one else would want to use the shower. She was fairly certain she was the only one who took advantage of the office shower and dressing room. The guys would just as soon wait until they got home to shower. She couldn't stand having dried paint on her. On the days she helped paint, she almost always showered before leaving the office.

She was glad one of the teams was shorthanded this afternoon. It gave her a chance to get away and do something other than sit at her desk and wonder how Peyton's lunch date had gone.

Margot Joseph.

"What does Peyton see in her?" she asked out loud.

Well, let's see...she's rich, she's famous, she's successful. She's attractive. And she's an arrogant bitch, she added.

She smiled at her reflection in the mirror. Did she really just call Margot Joseph a bitch?

"Yeah, I did."

She shook her head, hating the jealousy she felt. Peyton could go out with anyone she wanted to. And in turn, Logan could too. Only she didn't want to. She wanted...she just wanted to be with Peyton.

How did this happen?

She stared at her reflection again, meeting her gaze head on. Yes, how did it happen that her usual college girls held no interest for her anymore? There was only one answer: Peyton.

Well, it wouldn't do her any good hiding here in the office. She could always call up Staci and see if she wanted to get some dinner. But she knew where that would lead. No, better to pick up dinner and take it home. She grabbed her phone and headed out, thinking she'd call ahead and order some Mexican food. She was surprised to see a missed call from Peyton. She noted the time. After lunch. Susan must have mentioned that she'd been there. Or maybe Margot did.

She tapped the call back number, telling herself again that it was none of her business who Peyton went to lunch with, who she went out with. She had no holds on Peyton. They were only tiptoeing around dating, nothing more.

"Logan," Peyton answered. "I was afraid you weren't going to call me back."

"Sorry. I just now saw where you'd called. What's up?" she asked, hoping she sounded a little more nonchalant than she felt.

"Can you...come over?"

Logan's eyebrows shot up. That, she was not expecting. "Umm, I guess. Everything okay?"

"No. Everything is not okay." Peyton paused. "I want you to come over. I need...I want to break your no hanky-panky rule. If you want to, that is."

Logan laughed quietly. "You mean, like right now?"

"Yes. Right now."

Damn. Logan felt her pulse race at the thought of being with Peyton again. She didn't know if it was a good idea or not. Shouldn't they at least talk about Margot? Should she tell Peyton how she'd felt today when she saw Margot? Oh, hell, they could talk later.

"I'll be right there."

She raced out of the office and jumped into her Jeep, pulling away before she'd even put her seat belt on. She tried to obey the traffic laws, she really did. The last thing she wanted was to get stopped for speeding. That would only delay her seeing Peyton… Peyton and hanky-panky.

She laughed at their use of that word. It had started down at the coast, the night they watched the moon. Blankets and wine and she had promised Peyton there would be no hanky-panky. No, that happened the next night. And the truth was, that was the night her world changed.

She nearly skidded to a stop in Peyton's driveway, then she sat in the Jeep for a long moment, trying to calm her nerves. She couldn't believe how anxious she felt. She finally got out, then paused again before she rang the doorbell. It opened immediately.

"Took you long enough."

Logan laughed. "I broke traffic laws to get here."

Peyton drew her inside and closed the door. And locked it. With their hands clasped, Peyton led her up the stairs.

"Do we need to talk first?" Peyton asked from above.

"I hope you're not taking me to your bedroom to talk," she said.

"I'm sorry about lunch," Peyton said.

"So, you *do* want to talk?"

"No. I want to make love with you."

Logan stopped her at the top of the stairs, smiling. "Good. Then we'll talk later." She pulled her close to her body, nearly melting at the contact. It had been so very many months since Peyton had been in her arms, but as their bodies met, as their kiss turned heated, it felt like only yesterday.

Peyton's arms circled her neck, her fingers moving slowly through her hair. She pulled away enough to meet her gaze and Logan saw the dark fiery blue that she remembered.

"I've missed this," Peyton murmured as her mouth moved to Logan's ear. "I've missed you."

Logan's eyes closed as she pulled Peyton impossibly closer. God, yes. She hadn't realized just how much she'd missed Peyton. She found her mouth again, moaning into the kiss as Peyton's tongue danced with hers.

Peyton ended the kiss, then came back and kissed her once more before whispering "bed."

"If you insist," Logan said, not wanting to break contact even to get naked. They made quick work of their clothes, tossing them where they might. Peyton flung the covers off the bed, then pulled Logan down with her. Logan covered Peyton's body with her own, relishing the feeling of skin on skin.

"God, you feel good," Peyton said, pulling Logan's mouth to her own.

The hurried kisses of earlier were replaced by slow, passionate ones as Logan fitted herself between Peyton's thighs and Peyton's hands roamed her back. Logan's lips trailed to Peyton's neck, nuzzling and nibbling before moving lower. Her tongue raked across a nipple, causing Peyton to moan softly.

"I could just devour you," Logan murmured.

"Then please do," Peyton whispered.

Logan's mouth closed over her nipple and Peyton's hips arched against her. Logan straddled her thigh, shoving her own between Peyton's legs. She could feel her wetness and she pressed harder into her, leaving her breast and going back to her mouth. The kiss ended quickly as they both pulled away with the need to breathe.

"Please go inside me," Peyton said as she arched again, hard, against Logan's thigh.

Logan lifted away slightly, moving her hand between their bodies. She slipped easily into her wetness, filling her, feeling Peyton tighten around her fingers. Logan remained still, only moving her thumb in quick circles around Peyton's clit. Peyton's legs squeezed tightly, and Logan felt a steady pulse against her fingers.

"Don't stop," Peyton gasped.

Logan continued her ministrations with her thumb, bending down to capture a nipple in her mouth. Peyton was moaning loudly as Logan's tongue flicked Peyton's nipple in the same manner as her thumb was doing to her clit.

"Oh...*God*, Logan," Peyton breathed. "God, *yes*."

Peyton's hips bucked against her hand, and Logan released her nipple, smiling as Peyton cried out in pleasure. Only then did she move her fingers, pulling out slightly, then going back inside, deeper than before. Peyton's hips arched against her again, and Logan began a slow rhythm, in and out, the slick wetness of Peyton's arousal coating her hand.

"I can't...I can't possibly have...another," Peyton gasped as her hips continued to match Logan's strokes.

"Try," Logan whispered into her ear. "Picture my mouth on you, my tongue inside you. Because that's what I want to do next."

"No...that's what I want to do next," Peyton murmured. "I can't wait to taste you again."

"Oh, baby, me either," Logan said as her tongue snaked into Peyton's ear, bathing it, loving the quick moan from Peyton. "Yes, I can't wait for your tongue to be inside me," she said, her hand moving faster now, her own hips moving against Peyton's thigh, trying to get some relief herself.

She didn't have to wait long as Peyton's breath caught and her hips arched hard one last time, then she let out a near scream as her orgasm hit. Logan stilled her hand, leaving her fingers inside Peyton a moment longer, only pulling out when Peyton's body relaxed. Peyton was breathing hard in quick pants, and Logan leaned her head against Peyton's chest, trying to still her own heated body, giving Peyton time to recover.

"You're almost there, aren't you?"

"God, yes," Logan said.

Logan still straddled her thigh, and Peyton moved her hand between her leg and Logan. Logan gasped as Peyton's fingers brushed her clit. She rocked against them quickly, pressing down hard with each stroke. She barely had time to register the feel of Peyton's fingers when she climaxed. Her orgasm was quick and sharp, and she buried her face against Peyton's neck to stifle her scream.

She shifted slightly, taking her weight off Peyton, but their hands continued to touch, moving slowly across each other's skin. Peyton drew her up for a kiss, a slow, gentle kiss of lips moving lightly against lips, nothing more. When the kiss ended, their eyes met. Peyton smiled slightly and Logan did the same.

"Thank you for coming over."

"Thank you for inviting me."

"Have you had dinner?" Peyton asked.

"No." Logan's fingers brushed against Peyton's breasts, watching as her nipples hardened. "That's the last thing on my mind right now," she murmured.

"Do you...want to talk?"

Logan shook her head. "No. I just want...I just want to be with you. Like this." She met her gaze again. "Naked and touching."

Peyton smiled. "Okay. Can you stay the night?"

"Absolutely."

"Good. Then I'll offer breakfast in the morning."

Logan rolled to her side, resting on her elbows. "Deal." Then she arched an eyebrow questioningly. "So...the sex toy. Did you keep it?"

Peyton laughed. "Of course. And imagine my surprise to find it when I was unpacking. I never did figure out how you managed to hide it in my luggage. You never came into my room."

"No? Maybe I snuck in when you were showering," she said.

"I don't think so. If that had been the case, you would have joined me in the shower."

"True." Logan lowered her head, nibbled on her breast. "Maybe I got the cleaning lady to bring it in."

"Maybe your sister gave you a key to my room," Peyton countered.

Logan shook her head. "No way. Just giving me your room number was a big deal for her. She wouldn't dare give me your key." Logan kissed her again. "So...where is it?"

"It's close by," Peyton said. "Do you want it?"

"Can we?"

Peyton sat up and pulled out the drawer beside her bed, taking the vibrator out. She held it up. "Do you want to?"

Logan stared at it, then at Peyton. "Do you use it?" she whispered.

Their eyes held.

Peyton nodded. "Yes."

Logan tilted her head. "Do you…think of me when you use it?"

Peyton nodded again. "Yes."

Logan reached out and took it from her, then leaned closer for a kiss. She could already hear the change in Peyton's breathing.

"Yes. I want to use it."

CHAPTER THIRTY-SIX

"You don't really have to fix breakfast," Logan said as they made their way downstairs after a really, really long shower together.

"We missed dinner," Peyton reminded her.

"I know. But we're going to be late as it is, and you're not even dressed yet. I can pick something up on the way."

"Are you sure?"

"Yeah." Logan pulled Peyton closer. "I'd rather spend the next few minutes kissing than cooking."

Peyton's arms looped over her neck as she leaned in close, her body covered in nothing more than a thin robe. As if they hadn't spent most of the night making love, Logan responded to her touch. Peyton did as well and their light kiss turned passionate instantly.

"I can't seem to get enough of you," Peyton murmured against her lips.

Logan pressed her against the wall, one hand sneaking between them to cup her breast. Peyton's nipple was hard and she rubbed against it. She was aroused all over again and she slipped her thigh between Peyton's legs, feeling Peyton push against her.

"Do we have time?" she asked between kisses.

"I'm the boss. I can be late," Peyton said as her tongue rubbed against Logan's lower lip.

Logan sucked it into her mouth, moaning with Peyton as they tried to get closer still. She was about to slip her hand inside Peyton's robe when the doorbell rang, startling them. Both of their breaths came fast, both aroused. Their eyes held as they pulled apart, then Peyton straightened her robe and headed for the front door.

Logan leaned against the wall, trying to catch her breath. Damn, but she wanted to drag Peyton back up to the bedroom and not come down for at least an hour. She turned her head, wondering who would be at Peyton's door at this hour. Her eyes widened as she saw Peyton take an enormous bouquet of flowers from a delivery guy.

Peyton was simply staring at them, and the delivery guy stood there patiently waiting. Logan fished out some bills from her pocket and handed them to the guy, who snatched them up with a quick smile.

They were beautiful, Logan had to admit. And it didn't take a genius to know who they were from.

"Damn. Must have cost her a fortune to get them delivered at this hour," she said.

Peyton finally looked at her. "I'm sorry."

"Don't be. They're beautiful," she said.

Peyton sat the vase down on the entry table. She stared at the card. Logan's gaze went there as well. There was only one word written there—Margot.

Peyton turned to her, holding her gaze. "We…we never did talk, did we?"

"No."

Peyton tugged her robe a little tighter, her hands fidgeting as if stalling for time. Logan reached out, stilling them.

"You don't owe me an explanation, Peyton."

"Don't I?"

"No. You and Margot are dating," she said, feeling a stab of jealousy at her words. "It's perfectly normal for her to send you flowers."

Peyton shook her head. "We're not really dating, Logan. She just won't give up."

"No. Why would she? You're a very desirable...very beautiful woman, Peyton. Why would she give up?" Logan shrugged. "I mean, she's rich and powerful. A successful businesswoman. She can have anyone she wants." Logan swallowed, trying to lose some of the bitterness she felt. "And, as she informed me, she wants you. And she never loses."

"And, as I told her, I'm not prey," Peyton said.

They stared at each other for a long moment, then Logan looked away, her gaze darting around the room quickly.

"I should probably get going," she said. "Busy day today."

Peyton sighed but said nothing.

Logan nodded and turned to go, feeling a pain in her heart that she'd never felt before.

"Logan?"

She stopped and turned back to Peyton with raised eyebrows. Peyton walked closer, not stopping until they were touching. Peyton's arms circled her shoulders and pulled her into a kiss. Feeling her resistance vanish, Logan wrapped her arms around Peyton's waist, holding her closer. The kiss was slow, soft, with a gentleness to it that simply melted Logan where she stood. They kissed that way for several breathless moments before pulling apart. With eyes locked together, Peyton cupped Logan's face, fingers running along her cheek, her thumb brushing against the lips she'd just kissed. Logan trembled from her touch, but she didn't dare move.

Finally, Peyton's fingers fell away and she took a step back. Logan couldn't help but wonder if Peyton was telling her goodbye.

CHAPTER THIRTY-SEVEN

Peyton hadn't been out to lunch with her friend Tracie in a couple of months and had readily accepted her invitation, agreeing to meet her at a favorite Mexican food restaurant, one that she and Alicia used to frequent for lunch. She was surprised that the thought of Alicia no longer conjured up images of her and Vicky, naked, in her bed. That seemed like an eternity ago. Maybe she should call Alicia and make amends. She really needed to thank her. If not for her affair with Vicky, Peyton and Vicky might still be together. That was depressing to think about.

"I'm glad you were free," Tracie said. "We should do this more often."

"Yes. I love this place," she said as she ate a tortilla chip laden with green salsa. "How have you been? Are you still dating Lee Ann?"

Tracie shook her head. "No. It's been at least a month since we went out. We didn't have enough in common to sustain it. She *hated* the theater," she said with a laugh. "As you know, that's a passion of mine."

"Do you still have season tickets to the Zach?"

"Of course. I took Lee Ann to see *Les Miserables*, thinking she'd at least enjoy that play." She shook her head again. "But no. We only went out once more after that." She waved her hand dismissively. "Besides, the sex wasn't good enough to overlook her flaws."

Peyton said nothing, wondering when a dislike of the theater became a flaw. While she enjoyed a couple of performances each year at Zachary Scott, she wouldn't call it a passion of hers.

"So what about you? You must be quite giddy," Tracie said.

Peyton scooped up more salsa with a chip. "Oh?"

"I was surprised to hear that Margot was no longer dating Meredith Calhoun. Actually, I was more shocked to hear she was ready to settle down finally."

"Really? Who's the lucky girl?"

Tracie laughed. "Well, you, silly."

Peyton nearly spit her chip out. "Me?" She shook her head. "No, you're mistaken."

"Oh, no. That's all everyone's talking about. I even heard that she's accompanying you to your CPA banquet. Heather was saying that Margot was looking forward to being in public with you as a couple. A coming out of sorts."

Oh. Dear. God. Peyton blinked several times, trying to follow Tracie's conversation. It was all *who* was talking about? Good Lord, she hadn't even spoken to Margot since their lunch date. She hadn't even bothered to call and thank her for the flowers. She didn't want to encourage her in any way.

"Well, I think everyone's gossip is a bit premature," she said finally. "Margot and I aren't a couple. Far from it."

"Oh, I know it would be quite astonishing if she really did settle down. I mean, we *are* talking about Margot here," Tracie said with a laugh. "How flattering that she's chosen you. You wouldn't believe how many are envious of you. They are already wondering how soon it'll be before you move into her new house."

Peyton was literally at a loss for words. Thankfully, their lunch was served. She dug into her enchiladas with a vengeance, feigning a hunger she was no longer feeling.

When she got back to her office, she went purposefully to Susan's desk. "I need to see you."

Susan looked away from her monitor with raised eyebrows. "I'm in the middle of our monthly billing," she explained. "Can it wait?"

"No. I need to talk. And you're the closest thing I have to a best friend."

Susan smirked. "Really? I'm straight and happily married. Do you think I'm the most qualified to offer you advice when it comes to your women problems?"

Peyton blew out her breath. "Don't be difficult, Susan. I've just been told that not only am I in a relationship with Margot Joseph, I'm apparently about to move into her house."

"Really? I thought you hated her house."

"I'm *not* moving in with her," Peyton nearly snapped. She took a deep breath. "Can you please come into my office and listen and pretend to be interested while I rant?"

Susan pushed her chair back. "Of course. I suppose the billing can wait. You are the boss, after all."

"Yes. Try to remember that." Peyton rolled her eyes as she walked into her office. She *really* needed to find a best friend. Susan was right. How could she possibly relate to this situation?

But Susan sat down in one of the visitor's chairs and gave Peyton her full attention. Or so it seemed.

"I slept with Logan," she blurted out.

"I know. You already told me."

"No. I mean…again." She walked to the window and stared outside. "Two days ago. After my lunch with Margot. I asked her to come over that night."

"And?"

"And she stayed the night." Peyton turned around and smiled. "Being with her is absolutely incredible."

"Then what's the problem?"

"Margot is the problem. She had flowers delivered to my house that morning…just as Logan and I were…well, saying our goodbyes," she said, blushing slightly. "A huge vase. An assortment of flowers. It was quite beautiful," she admitted.

"Okay. So Margot is wooing you too."

"Wooing? Do people really say 'wooing' anymore?" She sat down in her chair. "Margot has made it clear to me that she intends to pursue me. Her word, not mine," she said. "But she doesn't do anything for me. There's not even a ripple of an attraction between us."

"And there is with Logan?"

"Oh, God. Logan makes me want to melt into a little puddle," she said with a laugh.

"Okay. So date Logan and not Margot."

"But is there even the possibility of a future with Logan? I mean, I like her a lot. She's fun. But do we really have enough in common to date? Do we fit in each other's life?"

"And Margot fits?"

"Yes, of course she fits. And she's apparently telling our friends that we're a couple. They're most likely placing bets on when I move in with her."

"Okay. So why are you even debating this? It sounds like Logan is who you would rather go out with," Susan said reasonably.

Peyton raised her hands questioningly. "But do I even know Logan? I mean, she dates college students. She's not looking for a relationship. She just wants to have fun," she said.

"So you're looking for a relationship then?"

Peyton stared at her. "Susan, I'm thirty-five years old. Every date I go out on should be considered looking for a long-term partner, shouldn't it? I'm too old to just date for the sake of dating." She paused. "Aren't I?"

Susan shook her head. "My God, I don't know if there's even hope for you. You're not sixty-five, Peyton. You're only thirty-five. Go out. Have fun. See where it takes you." Susan threw up her arms. "Go out with both of them. Find a third person. Go out with her too. Why limit it?"

Peyton narrowed her eyes. "You're being no help."

"Yes, well, I warned you." Susan stood, signaling an end to their conversation. "It sounds to me like Logan is the one you *want* to be with, you're just not sure if she's the one you *should* be with."

Peyton leaned her head back against her chair. "Yes. That's it exactly."

"So, my straight, happily married woman's advice is…go out with the one who makes you happy. Forget Margot. Don't go out with her again. She'll move on to someone else eventually."

"I can't. I already have a date scheduled with her. That damn CPA banquet," she said.

"Oh, yeah. You're running for president. I can't wait for it."

"Yes, whose bright idea was that?"

"I believe it was yours."

Peyton waved her away. "Go finish the billing. We've solved nothing here."

CHAPTER THIRTY-EIGHT

Logan leaned back in the patio chair, her legs stretched out in front of her. "I'm crazy about her," she said. "Which…well, is crazy."

Drew laughed and tipped her beer bottle in her direction. "About damn time some woman made you crazy."

"She's going to break my heart, you know."

"You don't know that. She appeared to be quite charmed by you."

Logan smiled. "Charmed? Yeah, we've got this…this thing between us. But I can't compete with Margot Joseph." Logan sat up. "You should have seen the flowers, Drew. It was a huge vase with thirty or forty different flowers in there."

"I doubt flowers is going to be the deciding factor here," Drew said.

"She drives a Mercedes. She's a face—a name—in the community. She's a professional. She's always impeccably dressed." She motioned to herself. "Look at me. I can't compete with that."

"Look, if Peyton is someone you think you could love, then don't let Margot get in the way. You are who you are, Logan. You're not Margot Joseph. You're the complete opposite of Margot Joseph."

"Yeah. But that's the type of woman Peyton dates."

"From what we saw, she enjoyed her time with us out on the lake. And Jay and I are as far from Margot Joseph as you are. She's obviously attracted to you. I say, just ask her out. Do what you do, be who you are...and see what happens. You can't change yourself to try to be someone you think she'd like. Peyton already likes you the way you are."

"Yeah. But what if it's just the sex? What if that's all she wants from me?"

"There could be worse things, Logan," Drew said with a laugh.

Logan grinned. "Yeah. I suppose so."

Drew was right, of course. She couldn't change who she was. She didn't *want* to change. She knew what she did want though. For the first time in her life, she wanted someone. Wanted to be with them, share things with them, talk to them, laugh with them, love them. She wanted all of that—and much more—with Peyton.

So she would take Drew's advice. She would simply ask Peyton out and see where it would go. But she would wait until Monday. She didn't want to take a chance of getting crushed this weekend, if Peyton already had plans with Margot. If that was the case, she'd rather not know about it. No, she'd rather stick her head in the sand and pretend that Peyton and Margot weren't dating.

CHAPTER THIRTY-NINE

Peyton stared at the flowers Susan held. For a brief moment, she thought perhaps they would be from Logan, but they were just...too much. Logan would never do that.

"Did you have a good weekend or what?" Susan asked. "This looks like a thank-you gift to me."

"Very funny. No, I have not seen or spoken to Margot."

"Then I guess you're right," Susan said. "She doesn't give up. Where would you like them?"

Peyton motioned to the credenza behind her. "I think this group is even larger than the ones she had delivered to the house last week," she said.

"Are you going to call her this time?" Susan asked as she handed her the card.

Can't wait to see you. Margot.

"Seeing as how we're supposed to go out Saturday night...I suppose I should." She held the card up. "Doesn't this seem odd? She's not called me or made any attempt to see me. Yet she's had flowers delivered twice now."

"Maybe she's giving you some space."

Peyton shook her head. "One thing I've learned about Margot, she's only concerned about herself. I'm sure it didn't even faze her that I told her I didn't want to date her. She's used to getting whatever and whoever she wants." She tossed the card on her desk. "My guess is, she's having her secretary send these."

"Well, they're pretty, I'll say that."

Peyton's gaze landed on them. Yes, they were. Beautiful, in fact. Only they were just flowers, nothing more. They conjured up no romantic feelings in her whatsoever. And as soon as the damn CPA banquet was over, she would tell Margot in no uncertain terms that she did not, would not, date her. The fact that she was using Margot for her own means was not lost on her. She did feel a twinge of guilt about that, but it fled quickly. Margot was looking out for her own interests, and Peyton was doing the same. Margot was, whether Peyton wanted to admit it or not, quite powerful in the business community. Her name and face were recognized. And if others, like her, thought Margot's law firm did nothing more than prey on insurance companies, it was overlooked. Everyone knew that Margot had a handful of successful business clients as well, not only hordes of accident victims hoping to cash in.

And I'm looking to cash in too, she thought. Being president of her professional organization would no doubt bring in new clients. In fact, Margot herself could bring her new clients. But Peyton didn't want to play that game. If she was elected president, so be it. If not, she wasn't going to lose any sleep over it.

A quick knock at her door brought her around and she turned, finding Logan standing there. She smiled at Logan's "Keep Austin Weird" T-shirt.

"Hey."

"Hey yourself."

"Am I interrupting?"

Peyton stood up. "Not at all. Come in."

Logan's smile faded as her gaze was drawn to the large bouquet of flowers. It was only then that Peyton saw the single rose Logan held.

"Damn. She sent you more flowers?"

Peyton walked closer to her, taking the rose. She brought it to her nose, inhaling the fragrance. "It's beautiful. Thank you."

Logan pointed at the bouquet. "No, that's beautiful."

"No. That's excessive." She held the rose up. "I like this much better."

Logan seemed to relax then and her smile returned. Peyton couldn't help herself as she leaned closer, kissing Logan softly on the mouth.

When she pulled away, Logan had a slight flush on her face.

"So…I came early," Logan said. "You know, in case someone else came by, wanting to take you to lunch."

She looked at her expectantly, but Peyton shook her head. "I can't. I have a lunch date with a client. How about tomorrow?"

"Can't. It's Mandy's birthday. I'm taking her out."

"Oh." *Who was Mandy?* "Well…"

"Mandy is my office manager," Logan explained. "How about dinner?"

"Tonight?"

"Yeah."

Peyton didn't hesitate. "Okay."

Logan grinned. "Good. I'll pick you up early. Six. Casual. Very casual." She glanced at Peyton's outfit. "And wear sensible shoes. The ones you wore to Mount Bonnell will work."

Before Peyton could ask any questions, Logan kissed her and was gone.

"Sensible shoes?" *Wonder where she's taking me now?*

* * *

"A picnic dinner?"

"And it involves hiking."

Peyton laughed. "Okay, so that's a first for me. Mount Bonnell again?"

"No, no. The 360 Bridge," she said. "Pennybacker." Logan glanced at her. "We'll catch the sunset. Nice views of Lake Austin too."

The October evening was pleasant, and they both wore jeans. Logan had on some lightweight hiking boots, but Peyton wore the lone pair of athletic shoes she owned. She raised her eyebrows skeptically when Logan parked near a No Parking sign.

"Yeah, so it's not really an official overlook," she said with a grin.

Peyton shook her head. "You're going to get towed."

"No, no. Two other cars here. People do this all the time." Logan got out and went around to the back of the Jeep, pulling out a picnic basket and a blanket.

Peyton still hesitated. "Are you sure it's okay?"

"Sure. It'll be fun," Logan said. "Come on. Sunset is around seven."

Peyton put her fears of getting towed and ticketed aside and followed Logan to a trail between the trees. It was a steep hike, and she held on to the junipers as her feet slipped on the rocks. But a mere ten minutes later they were at the top. And the view was breathtaking.

"Wow."

"Yeah. Pretty awesome, isn't it?"

Peyton turned in all directions, seeing the Austin skyline in the near distance, watching a boat speed by on the lake below, then turning to the west where the sun was already beginning to turn the landscape a gorgeous orange.

She took a deep breath, absorbing it all. How had she lived in this city for the better part of seventeen years and never even heard of this place? She glanced over at Logan, who was busy spreading out a blanket so they'd have an unobstructed view of the sunset. There were two other couples there, both with the same plan as them, apparently. One couple was sitting on some rocks near the edge. The other couple also had a blanket, but they were farther back against the trees.

Peyton joined Logan on the blanket, crossing her legs at the ankles and hugging her knees. She had a smile on her face as she watched Logan pull items from the basket, including a bottle of wine.

"Cheap sangria," Logan said. "To go with our tacos."

Paper plates, plastic forks, several foil-wrapped tacos and a tub of rice. A paper bag with grease stains contained fresh tortilla chips and a white Styrofoam cup held the salsa.

"But I did remember wineglasses this time," Logan said. "Well, sort of."

Peyton was completely charmed by Logan's picnic, plastic wine cups and all. And if they'd been alone, she would have leaned over and kissed her right then and there.

"It's nothing fancy," Logan said almost apologetically.

"I don't need fancy," she said as she picked up a cup and the bottle of sangria. "It's perfect like this."

And it was. It was a comfortable, companionable silence as they ate dinner, their gazes alternating between the approaching sunset and each other. Flirty smiles and accidental touches caused Peyton to wish they were truly alone. She had a need to be close to Logan, to touch her unabashedly, to kiss her. As their eyes found each other more often than the sunset, Peyton realized Logan was feeling the same. But quiet conversation from the other couples there made her resist her urges.

"It's pretty, isn't it?"

"Yes. Very," Peyton said as her gaze returned to the sunset.

"When I used to spend the summers here with Ted, when I was still a kid, he used to take me to Enchanted Rock," Logan said. "We'd sleep in a tent and do the whole camping thing. We'd always hike to the top of the rock to watch the sunset." She turned to Peyton. "And sometimes, if he could get me up, he'd haul my ass up there to catch the sunrise too."

"Is he where you got your love of this from?" she asked with a motion toward the sun.

"Yeah, I guess. I was always closer to my dad than my mom," Logan said. "Actually, Emma is closer to my mother than I am."

"You were five when they married?"

"Yeah. Emma is just a little older. She was the girlie girl my mother always wanted. I just didn't fit that mold," Logan said with a laugh. "What about you? You said you had one sibling?"

Peyton nodded. "An older sister. Six years apart." She sighed. "We're not close at all though. We call on birthdays, that's about it."

"Where does she live?"

"Waco. That's where I grew up," she said. "My parents divorced when I was a senior in high school. Beth was already married." She shrugged. "I moved to Austin to go to college and we kinda drifted apart. The whole family did."

"That's too bad. I can't imagine my life without Emma. My dad and I are close. My mother, well, we're not emotionally close, but that's not to say we don't talk," Logan said.

"My father remarried and lives in Phoenix now," she said. "I've met his wife only once. And my mother, well, the divorce took its toll on her." Peyton shook her head. "She was never the same. She became overly religious. When I came out to her, you'd have thought the world was coming to an end," she said with a laugh. She could speak lightly of it now. At the time, she was devastated by her mother's reaction. They too had just drifted apart.

"Yeah. Some parents are only concerned with how that news affects them, not their children," Logan said.

"Exactly. I needed her support," she said. "I was scared, I was lonely. But I got nothing from her. My sister was accepting, but we still weren't close."

Logan reached over and pulled her into a one-armed hug, then released her. "I don't like to think of you being lonely," she said quietly.

Peyton met her eyes in the waning twilight. "Sometimes... I'm still lonely."

As their eyes held, she swore she felt something pass between them. She wanted to hold on to it tightly, and her gaze never wavered.

"We should...we should probably get going," Logan said. "Because right now, I really want to kiss you."

Peyton nodded. "Will you stay with me tonight? Will you make love with me?"

Logan smiled, a sweet smile that dissolved any loneliness she may have been feeling. "I'll love you all night long if you'll let me."

Peyton reached out, tangling her fingers with Logan's. "Yes. I'll let you."

CHAPTER FORTY

Peyton finished up the account she was working on, then decided the other two that needed her attention could wait until later. Her focus just wasn't on them.

She spun around in her chair, staring outside her window, thinking again that she had to tell Logan she was going out with Margot on Saturday night. She'd put it off all week, even though they'd seen each other twice. She just couldn't find the right words to say. It wasn't really a date, she kept telling herself. But to Margot, it was. And to Logan, it certainly would be. She tried to reason that it was okay that she went out with Margot. For all she knew, Logan was still seeing Staci or any other of her college-age friends. Of course, she didn't really believe that. Logan had given her no indication that she was seeing—dating—anyone else.

A quick smile came to her face as she accepted the fact that she and Logan *were* dating, were seeing each other. She enjoyed every minute, every second of the time they spent together. But her smile faded as quickly as it had come. Saturday night. Surely Logan would want to do something. And then Peyton would have to tell her, would have to tell her she couldn't. Because she was going out with Margot Joseph. And Logan would be hurt.

The ringing of her phone brought her attention back to her desk. She picked it up, seeing Jay Burns' name. They'd exchanged phone numbers the day Peyton had joined them at the lake, but she hadn't spoken to her since then.

"Hello, Jay. How are you?"

"Hi, Peyton. I hope I'm not catching you at a bad time," Jay said.

"No, not at all."

"Good. I wanted to see if you were free on Saturday evening. The forecast is sunny and warm so we're having steaks out by the pool. An early dinner. We'd love for you to join us."

Peyton leaned her head back on her chair and closed her eyes. "I'm sorry, Jay. I would love to, but I've got plans on Saturday." She opened her eyes again, realizing how that sounded. "I've got a CPA banquet to go to. It's our annual dinner," she explained.

"Oh, that's too bad. When I mentioned dinner, Logan was hoping you'd come. I guess she forgot about your—"

"Actually, I don't think I mentioned it to her," she said, allowing herself a small lie. "I'd love to see you and Drew again though. Perhaps another time?"

"Of course. We'll look forward to seeing you."

"Thanks, Jay. We'll talk soon."

She held her phone tightly in her lap, trying to decide what she was going to tell Logan. She should call her. Explain.

No. Not over the phone. That would be the cowardly way out. She would simply tell her the truth. It was no big deal, really. Logan would understand. Surely, she would.

Although an hour later, as Logan stood in her office, that flirty, sexy smile on her face, Peyton wasn't so sure.

"I was in the area," Logan said. "Honestly."

Peyton smiled, unable to take her eyes off Logan.

"And I'm not even here to steal you away for lunch."

"Oh?"

"Yeah. I just wanted to see you," Logan said. "And to invite you to dinner Saturday night. Jay and Drew want to do steaks out by the pool."

Peyton's heart sunk. "Actually, Jay already called me."

"She did? Oh, well, great," Logan said. "I forgot she had your phone number."

Peyton walked around her, closing the door. When she turned back around, she moved closer to Logan, letting her hand touch Logan's arm, squeezing lightly. "I can't make it, though," she said. "I've...I've got this...this CPA banquet."

"Oh. Okay."

The disappointment was evident in Logan's voice, on her face. She rushed to explain.

"It's our annual dinner and meeting," she said. "I'm running for president. It's kind of a big deal."

"Really? Wow." Logan's smile returned. "Need a date?"

Peyton simply stared at her, not knowing what to say. Apparently she didn't have to say anything.

"Oh. You already have one," Logan said. "You...you haven't mentioned Margot in a while. I thought—"

"Logan, this was planned a long time ago. Margot...she's a name in the community. She's well respected. Everyone knows her or at least knows of her." She waved her hand nervously in the air. "TV commercials, billboards," she said.

"Hey, no problem," Logan said. "Margot's a perfect date for you. Me, I wouldn't have a thing to wear."

"Logan, it's...it's not really a date," she said lamely.

"Sure it is. But it's none of my business."

"Logan—"

Logan held her hand up. "You don't owe me an explanation, Peyton."

"I'm not...I'm not sleeping with Margot," she said. "I'm not even dating her. This is something that was planned before you and I—"

A loud knock on her door stopped her explanation. Susan opened her door and stuck her head in, meeting her questioning gaze.

"Just wanted to let you know that...Margot just pulled up out front." Her glance went to Logan, then back to her. "I thought..." she said with a shrug.

Oh, dear God.

"Yeah, thanks," Logan said. "I was just leaving."

Susan closed the door again, and Peyton grabbed Logan's hand. "Logan, please. Don't go."

Logan's smile was forced. "Really, it's okay," she said. "Call me if you want to get together. Whenever."

Peyton looked desperately at her, but Logan was already opening the door. Peyton then heard Margot's voice, heard Logan and Margot exchange what she assumed was a greeting. She turned around, facing the window, hating herself at that moment. She'd hurt Logan, she knew that. She should have told her earlier about the banquet. She shouldn't have tried to hide it from her.

"You free for lunch?"

And the hits keep coming.

Peyton turned around, facing Margot. The smile that Margot gave her was as forced as Logan's had been. Peyton joined the crowd, forcing one as well.

"Sure."

CHAPTER FORTY-ONE

"I'm overreacting, aren't I?"

Jay nodded. "Maybe a little."

"It's just…Margot Joseph is so phony. I don't get it. What does Peyton see in her?"

"I spent quite a bit of time with Margot when we were designing her house," Jay said. "I know she wanted it to be a showcase more than anything else." She shook her head. "Reminded me of the mansion I used to live in."

"Your ex? Katherine?"

"Yes." Jay glanced over to the grill where Drew was readying it for the steaks for their early dinner. "Margot reminds me of Katherine a lot. Charming, although there's nothing sincere about it. Everything is for a purpose. *Their* purpose. Katherine was an attorney too, you know."

Logan nodded. "Yeah. And the Peyton I know could see through that. I can't see her being charmed by that type of person."

"Well, we were only around her at the lake, but she seemed very down to earth. I don't see her with that crowd that Margot hangs with."

"I know. Yet that's her type," she said.

"But you two, you're dating. Right?"

Logan shrugged. "Yes. I mean, I think so. We go out. We… we sleep together."

"Then I think you're overreacting to this alleged date she has with Margot. Do you have reason to think that she'd lie to you?"

"No."

"So this banquet was planned months ago, I'd imagine. And months ago, she *was* dating Margot. From what you've told us, this is more of a business arrangement than a social date."

"Yeah. I keep telling myself that. Because the thought of her being with Margot makes me want to vomit. But then I keep seeing Margot in her office, all dressed up and coming to take her to lunch. And Margot had that arrogant smirk on her face as I was leaving." Logan reached for the beer that Drew handed her. "Thanks." She turned back to Jay. "Margot always gets what she wants. She told me that in no uncertain terms."

"Yeah," Drew said. "But what do you want?"

"I think we both want the same thing," she said. "Peyton."

"And probably for two completely different reasons."

Jay leaned across the table and squeezed her arm affectionately. "How far in are you?"

Logan smiled. "I'm afraid I'm too far in."

Jay smiled too. "Good. About time you fell in love with someone."

"Yeah. But what if it's the wrong someone?"

"These things have a way of working out." Jay glanced at Drew and smiled. "Don't they, sweetheart?"

Drew nodded. "Yes, they do." Drew looked at Logan. "I told you about when we were in Hawaii. I was crazy in love. And that morning when Katherine came back and took Jay away, I was a mess. I wanted to believe that Jay could see through the façade, but a part of me was so scared she wouldn't." She smiled at Jay. "Unwarranted fear, it turns out."

Jay laughed. "I do believe we had sex on the beach that night."

Drew laughed too and glanced at Logan. "And we're not talking about the drink."

Logan held her hands up. "Too much information right there."

She watched them, their eyes still lighting up when they looked at each other. And it was with envy that she watched Drew lean over to kiss Jay. These were her two best friends and they were always affectionate with each other. She had been around them for years, but this was the first time that she realized how much she wanted what they had. Before Peyton came into her life, she hadn't given it much thought. She was content dating college students. They were fun. They weren't looking for anything other than a good time. There were no commitments, no responsibilities. She hadn't considered she would meet someone completely different and fall head over heels in love.

And they were different. And Peyton was out right now with Margot Joseph, someone who was not different. Margot sent her expensive flowers and took her to fancy restaurants. Margot knew all the right people, said all the right things. The car she drove symbolized her personality and her prominence in the world. A status symbol for all to see.

She supposed the Jeep she drove was a status symbol too. Only it served to illustrate how completely opposite she and Margot Joseph were. And in the middle of them was Peyton. Logan had a sudden ache in her heart. Peyton would never choose her. Not over Margot Joseph. Who would?

CHAPTER FORTY-TWO

Peyton stared at herself in the mirror. Her slate gray skirt and cobalt blouse looked as striking as the salesperson had said it would. "It'll just pop with the color of your eyes." Only her eyes appeared lifeless at the moment. When the door to the restroom opened, she looked away from the mirror—and her own accusing gaze—and smiled politely at the woman who'd entered.

Once back in the ballroom, she scanned the crowd, seeing familiar faces, most of whom she only saw once or twice a year. A profound sadness settled over her.

What am I doing here?

She'd not heard a word from Logan since she'd left her office. Not that she expected to. Logan had said to call her if she wanted to get together. It was only two days, but she missed her like crazy. She just hadn't dared to pick up the phone to call her. Because honestly, she didn't know what to say to her. She would wait until after the weekend, after this *stupid* banquet was over with.

Lunch with Margot had been strained to say the least. While Margot never once mentioned Logan or even asked what she'd been doing at Peyton's office, her demeanor made it clear that she was perturbed to find Logan there. Peyton saw no reason to offer an explanation. Logan had as much right to be there as Margot did. More so, in fact. She was sleeping with Logan, not Margot.

Yet here she was, all dressed up, with Margot as her date, not Logan. The complicated mess her life was in right now was her own doing, all because she thought she needed to make an impression on her peers and colleagues. And to what end? To be elected president? As if that would be a defining moment in her career? Her firm wasn't large, but it was large enough for her. She knew the real reason she'd thought she needed to add something to her professional résumé. She was simply unfulfilled in her personal life so she had turned her focus on her career, even though she was already satisfied with the track her professional life had taken.

She drew in a heavy breath, something she'd been doing a lot lately. She had simply been dreading this evening. She looked down at her arm, seeing the dozens of twinkling diamonds flashing at her—the bracelet that Margot had slipped on her wrist earlier.

"There's only one thing missing," Margot had said.

Peyton had looked at her questioningly.

Margot had produced an elegant black box. Peyton had been too stunned to offer a protest.

"You're a beautiful woman, Peyton. You deserve beautiful things."

And now here they were, mingling with her colleagues, Margot playing the crowd as only she could do. Peyton looked across the throng of people, finding Margot, her suit very similar to her own. Margot's words were still fresh in her mind.

"You look stunning," she'd said. "I think we'll be the sharpest looking couple there."

Peyton hated to admit it, but Margot had been right. They matched perfectly. But as she stared out over the crowd, her gaze traveling past Margot to the others in the room, she felt as lost and…and depressed as she could ever remember feeling.

God, I hate my life.

That one thought hit home to her like no other. Yes, right now, she simply *hated* her life. This is not where she wanted to be. These people were not who she wanted to be with. Margot was not the person she wanted as her date.

She felt her chest tighten, felt an acute dose of anxiety hit. No. This is *not* where she wanted to be. Before she could change her mind, before she could come to her senses, she walked purposefully toward Margot. She was involved in an animated conversation with Randal Milstead, the current president of the organization. Peyton didn't consider waiting for a break in their exchange.

"May I speak with you, please?" she asked quietly.

Margot glanced her way and nodded. "Of course."

Peyton smiled apologetically at Randal, then led Margot toward the doors. Margot followed but hesitated when Peyton walked outside.

"I think they're about to serve dinner," Margot said.

"I know. This won't take long."

Margot's smile was forced. "What's wrong, Peyton?"

Peyton held up her wrist, showing the bracelet. "For starters, this. I can't accept it," she said.

"Of course you can."

"No, Margot, I can't." Peyton fumbled with the clasp, finally releasing it. She held it out to Margot. "I can't accept it."

Margot's smile bordered on condescending as she took the bracelet from her. "You're a beautiful woman, Peyton. I can give you beautiful things." She laughed quietly. "Your painter friend… well, I found out she doesn't really own the business. Her father does. She's more like an…an office manager, that's all." Her laugh was smug this time. "Look what she drives."

Peyton was at a loss for words, so surprised was she that Margot would bring up Logan.

Margot held the bracelet up, the light making the diamonds twinkle. "She can't give you expensive things like this. I can. I can give you the moon, Peyton."

Peyton stared at the bracelet, then brought her gaze back to Margot. She shook her head slowly. "The moon? No. You can give me everything *but* the moon," she said. "Logan…has given me a full moon, a midnight moon as seen over the surf at high tide, as seen from atop Mount Bonnell." She smiled at the confused expression on Margot's face. "You see, Logan offers me nothing but herself…and the moon. You offer me everything *but* yourself," she said, motioning to the diamonds.

Margot frowned. "The moon?"

"I know you think this is some game, some competition. I know you're used to having anyone, anything, you want. I'm not interested in that with you. I'm sorry."

Margot smirked. "You were interested enough to sleep with me."

"Actually, no. I was jealous enough to sleep with you," she said. "It was the night I ran into Logan again."

Margot's face hardened. "Logan and the young blonde she was with."

"Yes."

"Well, I suppose I'm willing to forgive you for that," Margot said. "I was sleeping with Meredith at the time." She fingered the bracelet. "All of that aside, I'm ready to talk about us."

Peyton looked at her incredulously. "There is no *us*, Margot. Haven't you heard anything I've said?"

Margot's smile was patronizing. "And haven't you heard what I've said? I can give you anything…everything. We'd be good together. Look at us," she said, motioning between them. "A perfect couple."

"All of this means nothing to me," Peyton said. "I convinced myself that it did. For years, I thought this," she said, motioning to Margot and her bracelet, "was important. There were all these rules, you see. Rules that I thought I had to follow." She shook her head. "I always thought this was what I wanted."

"What are you talking about?"

"I'm talking about us. I'm talking about the way we live. I'm talking about the prestige that we place on things and people. It's all so…so ludicrous," she said. "What I really want has been right in front of me."

"You're making no sense, Peyton."

"I don't care about this damn banquet and being president. I don't care about a diamond bracelet, Margot. I don't care about things you can give me. It means nothing if you're not happy. And I just want to be happy. I want to be fulfilled." She tapped her chest. "In here. That's what I'm talking about. And Logan makes me happy. Logan makes me feel like I'm the most precious person in the world."

"She's a nobody," Margot said. "She's a painter."

"I don't care what she does for a living. I don't care if her name is attached to that business or not. All she does is bring me a single rose and offer me the moon. Literally. She's like a breath of fresh air." She stared at Margot. "And I'm acting like she's not good enough. You're trying to convince me that she's not good enough."

"She's *not* good enough. You deserve someone better than that."

Peyton met her gaze. "You? I deserve you?"

"Yes. We can be good together."

"Good? How? We have nothing in common, Margot."

"Of course we do. We travel in the same circle, Peyton."

"Then I need a new circle," she said. "The truth is, I'm not attracted to you. I'm not interested in any kind of a romantic relationship with you. I'm sorry if I led you to believe that."

Margot took a step back. "If you think I'm giving up, you're crazy."

"I told you once, I'm not prey."

"I don't consider you prey, Peyton. Just a very enticing challenge. I always get what I want."

"Is that a threat?"

"I'm just saying, I can be very persuasive. I can give you things, Peyton. I can also take them away."

The smile Margot gave her sent a shiver down her spine.

"So that *is* a threat, then," she said.

"I have a lot of influence, as you know. Which is why you wanted me to accompany you to your banquet this evening. Because I have influence." She shrugged. "I don't mind you using me, Peyton. I just expect something in return."

"Sex?"

"That's a good start," Margot said with a smile. "But I'm getting older. I'm ready to settle down. You and I would make a great team."

Peyton couldn't believe what she was hearing. "You're crazy," she said, speaking the first words that popped into her mind. "I'm not something you can buy, Margot."

"I think you forget the position of prominence that I hold within our circle of friends and colleagues. I can easily have you shunned from the group. I would hate to see your business suffer."

Peyton laughed. "If you think my business stays afloat only because of the few clients I have from our 'circle,'" she said, making quotation marks in the air, "you're very mistaken."

"Well, we can discuss business later, Peyton. We should really get back inside. I'm sure you're anxious to go mingle."

Peyton stared at her. "I'm truly at a loss here, Margot. I feel like I'm talking to a…a robot or something."

"I don't understand."

"Let me put it to you simply. I'm in love with someone. And it's not you. So I'm not going back inside with you. I'm not going to lunch with you. I'm not doing *anything* with you ever again. Understand?"

"In love?" Margot scoffed. "Please. What does love have to do with it? I'm talking about a business arrangement, Peyton. One that would benefit both of us."

"I know what you're talking about. And it's sad that you don't realize how ridiculous that sounds," she said. "I'm not interested. Take your offer somewhere else." She walked back toward the door. "I'm sorry, Margot, but I can't do this."

"Do this? We're already here. It's started. You're going to be president," she said.

"I don't care. I'm not staying. I'm sorry that I've wasted your time this evening."

Margot squared her shoulders. "You're making a big mistake, Peyton."

"No. I'm finally doing the right thing," she said. "I'm following my heart."

"And it will get you nowhere," Margot said. "Talk about not having anything in common, that's you and your young friend, Logan."

"You're wrong. We have a lot in common. I was just too blind to see it." She took another step toward the door, then stopped. "I'm sorry, Margot. Really, I am."

Margot raised her chin and walked past Peyton to the door, opening it. "When you come to your senses, give me a call. My offer might still be on the table."

"No thanks."

Margot's strained smile turned mocking. "One day you will look back on this moment and realize you made the wrong choice."

"Regardless if Logan is the wrong choice or not...you would never have been the right one."

And, as if not wanting her to get in the final jab, Margot tossed a rather lame parting shot over her shoulder.

"Your loss, Peyton."

Peyton very nearly rolled her eyes. "What did I ever see in her?" she murmured.

She then realized that people were looking at her. She went back inside, heading to their table. Her whole staff was there. Susan and Michael, Ingrid and Paul, and Maria and Roberto. She smiled apologetically at them even as Margot took her seat at the table. She bent down, whispering to Susan.

"I've got to go. Please, can I take your car?"

Susan's eyebrows shot up. "What? No. It's starting. You're running for president."

"I don't care."

Susan glanced at Margot. "What's going on?"

"I've got to find Logan."

"Are you crazy? Dinner is about to be served."

"Okay, yes. I'm crazy. Crazy in love," Peyton said. She looked at Margot, who had her back to them. "Please, I'll leave your car at my house. Maria or Ingrid can give you a ride."

Susan shook her head. "No. You're supposed to give a speech."

"You wrote it. You give it," she said. "Please? I need your car."

Susan fumbled in her purse. "You owe me," she said as she handed Peyton her keys. "Keep the keys and lock it. Michael has a set."

Peyton grinned. "You're the best." She bent down and quickly kissed Susan on the cheek. "Remind me to give you a raise."

"Count on it."

As she headed for the doors, she felt eyes on her, and she turned, seeing curious glances directed her way. She imagined she heard whisperings as she made her escape. She didn't care. She only had one thing on her mind and that was finding Logan.

Of course, it would have helped had Susan told her where they'd parked. She pushed the remote several times, looking for flashing lights.

"Come on, come on," she murmured as she snaked her way through the parking lot. Finally, the lights on a Toyota Camry came on, and she hurried toward it.

The drive to her house was made without thought, her hands tight on the steering wheel. She called Logan once, but there was no answer. She parked on the side of her driveway and locked Susan's car. Once inside her house, she ran up the stairs as fast as her heels would allow. She stripped out of her suit and tossed it on the bed, then hurried to her closet, pulling out the first pair of jeans she saw. She added a T-shirt and sneakers and sprinted down the stairs again.

She was out of breath when she picked up her phone and called Logan again. Her heart was pounding nervously as it went unanswered…again.

"Please, Logan," she whispered to no avail as it went to voice mail. She ended the call without leaving a message. She would simply have to find her.

But as she started her car and backed out of the garage, she realized she had no idea where she was going. To Drew and Jay's? Did she even remember how to get out there? She tapped the steering wheel with her fingers, trying to decide what to do. She pulled her phone out, flipping through her contacts. She stared at Jay's name. They had dinner planned. Surely Logan was still there.

"But she didn't answer her phone," she murmured. Maybe Logan didn't want to talk to her, didn't want to see her.

She tapped Jay's name anyway. She had to find Logan.

CHAPTER FORTY-THREE

Logan sorted through the pile of rocks she'd collected, finding a larger one. She held it in her hand, then tossed it into the lake, hearing the splash. She could just barely make out the ripples as they hit the pier. She looked up. She was far enough from the city to see the stars, but the moon was rising and it lit up the sky.

And that, of course, made her feel…well, a little gloomy. She would forever associate the moon with Peyton. While she liked a good sunset, even a nice sunrise, the full moon was something special. She remembered the first time her father had dragged her out of a warm sleeping bag to hike to a rise to see the moon as the clock ticked near midnight. And she remembered when he bought this place. She'd still been in high school. But that first summer, on the full moon of each month, he'd take her out on the boat and they'd float lazily on the lake, watching as it hovered overhead. Carefree times, for sure. She'd gotten her love of the quiet, of the night sky, from her father. And she'd never shared that with anyone.

Not until that night at the coast when she'd banged on Peyton's door, coaxing her out to share the high tide and the midnight moon with her. Logan wondered if she hadn't fallen in love with Peyton that very night.

"And she's out with Margot Joseph tonight," she said dryly.

So sure, maybe it had been planned a while ago—this date. Logan tried to remind herself that she had no holds on Peyton. They were dating, they were getting to know each other. They weren't in a relationship.

She grabbed another rock and tossed it into the lake. No, they weren't in a relationship. What the hell did she know about relationships anyway? She had no experience in anything other than dating college girls. Peyton was a mature woman used to dating women...well, women like Margot Joseph.

"I am *so* not Margot Joseph," she murmured as she reached for the wine bottle, taking a long swallow.

Maybe...maybe she and Peyton *were* too different. Maybe they didn't have enough in common to make this into something. So what if the sex was fantastic? Was that enough?

She took another rock and tossed it in the lake, the splash disturbing the silence. She inhaled deeply, enjoying the fragrance of the old juniper that guarded the pier. Yes, the sex was something special. That didn't necessarily mean their relationship would be as well. She let out a frustrated sigh and lay back on the pier, arms out to her sides. She stared up into the heavens, wishing she could turn her thoughts to something other than Peyton... and Margot.

But they continued to dance around in her head, making her crazy. She closed her eyes to the stars, picturing instead sunshine and sand, racing waves on the beach, the roar of the surf, the cry of the gulls—all things that would forever be linked to Peyton. But still, it was a peaceful feeling that washed over her. Because she could see the look in Peyton's blue eyes, the look she had after they made love. The look that told her it was more than sex. It was making love.

She opened her eyes again, blinking into the night sky, focusing again on the stars. She rolled her head to the side, finding the moon as it rose higher into the sky. Peyton's eyes couldn't lie. She smiled slightly. No, those eyes didn't lie.

She sat up and grabbed another rock, giving it an easy toss into the lake. So maybe she had overreacted. As Jay had said, it was a business date. Probably. No reason for her to be riddled with jealousy. No reason to act like a damn spoiled child and run and hide from Peyton.

"You feel like company?"

Logan jumped, nearly falling off the pier and into the lake. "Jesus, you scared the crap out of me!"

"Sorry." The boards of the pier creaked as Peyton walked closer. "Can I join you?"

Logan nodded, wondering if she was dreaming that Peyton was here. What about her banquet? What about her date?

"You looked lost in thought," Peyton said as she sat down beside her. "Share?"

Logan shrugged. "A lot of things, really. At first, I was thinking that maybe you were right."

"Right about what?"

"Down at the coast, you said that I wasn't your type." She held up the wine bottle. "You wouldn't find Margot Joseph drinking wine out of the bottle."

"No." Peyton swung her legs into motion over the edge of the pier, and Logan found herself doing the same. "No, you wouldn't. You wouldn't find her sitting out here either."

Logan took a sip of the wine and handed the bottle to Peyton. The smile Peyton gave her nearly melted her heart.

"So what are you doing out here anyway? What happened to your banquet?"

Peyton tucked the wine bottle between her legs, then continued to swing them back and forth over the water. The silence was broken by the sound of an owl in the trees behind them.

"I decided I didn't want to be president," Peyton said.

"Really? I thought that was a big deal," she said.

"Oh, I don't know. It might bring in more business, but we're doing okay."

Logan leaned closer and bumped her shoulder. "What really happened?"

Peyton sighed. "Margot gave me a diamond bracelet."

Logan glanced at her wrists. They were bare. She reached out, rubbing her index finger against Peyton's skin. "Where is it?"

"I didn't accept it." Peyton cleared her throat. "She said she could offer me expensive things. She sends me huge bouquets of flowers, but all I want is a single rose," Peyton said, her voice soft and quiet, mixing with the stillness of the lake. "She said she could offer me the moon." Peyton turned, finding Logan's eyes in the moonlight. "I told her you had already given me the moon."

Logan was afraid to breathe, but she was not afraid to tell Peyton what was in her heart. "Peyton," she whispered. "Please… please say I'm not the only one."

"The only one?"

"To fall in love."

Peyton leaned forward, lightly kissing Logan's lips. "Sweetheart, I'm so in love with you. Crazy in love."

Logan blinked her eyes stupidly at her. "Really?"

Peyton laughed. "Yes, really."

"Wow. I'd practically had you and Margot married already," she teased.

Peyton slapped playfully at her arm. "Stop."

Logan felt giddy as she leaned into Peyton, kissing her again. She pulled back before it went any farther.

Peyton rested her head against Logan's shoulder. "I'm really sorry about the other day. I didn't mean to hurt you."

"Yeah. That stung."

"I didn't know how to tell you about the banquet. And Margot, yes, she's made it clear she wants more from me than friendship."

"I understand."

"I don't think you do." Peyton lifted her head, cupping Logan's face with one hand. "I don't want anything from her. To me, she's no different than Vicky, than any of the others in our so-called circle," she said. "After I met you, that circle that I called my friends, the women that I started dating, they all paled in comparison. And I didn't think I would ever see you again."

"I begged Emma to give me your name and address, but she refused," Logan said.

"Maybe it is fate then."

"Maybe."

Peyton leaned her head against her shoulder once again. "I feel so comfortable with you, Logan. It's so different from anything I've experienced before. It's a little scary."

"It's a lot scary." Logan linked her fingers with Peyton's. "So how did you find your way out here, anyway?"

"Jay. She texted me directions," Peyton said. "I really like her."

Logan laughed. "She's the only reason I didn't crash your banquet tonight. She convinced me I was overreacting."

"Jay and I are going to be good friends."

"That's great."

Peyton lifted her head and kissed her cheek. "I'm really sorry. How can I make it up to you?"

"Well, now that's a silly question," Logan murmured as her mouth met Peyton's. She let the kiss take her away, not even trying to temper things any longer. Peyton said she was in love with her. Did it get any better than that?

"So your father's not here, right?" Peyton whispered against her lips.

"He is *so* not here," Logan said as she lowered Peyton to the pier, her kisses hungry and demanding.

"And do you have a bedroom here?"

Logan smiled as she leaned up on her elbows. "What are you suggesting?"

"A bed."

Logan laughed. "Afraid we'll fall into the lake?"

"Yes."

CHAPTER FORTY-FOUR

Peyton bobbed in the water, holding tightly to the ski rope. Logan, with Drew and Jay in the boat, looked at her expectantly. She finally gave them the signal that she was ready. As soon as the weather had warmed, Logan had begun teaching her to ski. It was quite an exciting day when she got up for the first time. She hadn't lasted long before she crashed, but she was hooked. She relaxed now as Logan put the boat in motion, letting the boat pull her up. She wobbled to the side and almost fell but regained her balance. She laughed joyfully, and water sprayed around her as her skis cut through the water.

Never in a million years would she have believed the turn her life had taken. After months of juggling their time between Logan's duplex and her house, they decided it was time for a move. And while she loved her house, namely her pool and the location, it wasn't where she wanted to start her new life with Logan. So after going back and forth, trying to decide if it was too soon or not to look for their own house, fate took control again. An older home on Lake Travis came up for sale. It needed some work. Okay, it needed a *lot* of work, but the price was right. They'd snatched it up and had spent the spring remodeling. They still weren't finished, but they had officially moved in. The commute to work was long for both of them, but it was only twenty minutes from Drew and Jay's place and only ten minutes from Ted's weekend home. Tax season had been long and brutal, and she was actually thankful she'd not been elected president at the CPA banquet. She planned to spend the next few months getting her office at home set up so that she could work there a few days each week.

"You're doing great!" Jay yelled as Peyton crossed over the wake and to the other side of the boat.

Peyton laughed, but it was as if Jay's words hexed her. In a flash, she lost her balance and crashed into the lake headfirst, losing one of her skis. She swam over to retrieve it. Logan was circling around in the boat. Peyton floated on her back, waiting.

She looked up into the clear blue sky, a contented smile on her face. She absolutely loved living on the lake. She thought she would miss her pool. It was the one thing she used almost daily. But the clear lake waters had beckoned, and she and Logan swam most evenings after work.

"You okay?"

"Yep. Great fun," she said as she held onto the side of the boat. "Who's next?"

"I'll take a turn," Drew said.

Jay helped Peyton back into the boat, and she sat down beside her and toweled off. Aware of Logan's eyes on her, she turned, meeting her smile.

"You looked pretty good out there," Logan said.

"Thank you."

"Of course, the bikini helps," Logan added with a wink.

Peyton laughed and turned back to Jay. "She's got me skinny-dipping in the lake now," she said. "I think I love it more than she does."

Jay squeezed her arm affectionately. "I never thought I'd see Logan this happy."

"I never thought *I'd* be this happy," she said.

"Logan tells me you and Ted have hit it off."

Peyton laughed. "Logan is a carbon copy of her father. We have a standing dinner date with him once a week now."

"Here we go!"

Peyton leaned back as Logan revved the boat quickly, pulling Drew up on her one ski. She was quite good. Peyton hoped by the end of summer, she'd be able to slalom too. She relaxed, her gaze going from Drew to Jay and then to Logan. Her life had changed so much in the last year. Logan's best friends were now hers too. And while she still occasionally had lunch dates with women from her old circle, she now knew how little she'd had in common with them.

As for Margot, she hadn't seen or spoken to her since that night of the banquet. She'd heard Margot and Meredith had resumed their relationship. She'd also heard Meredith was sporting a *very* expensive diamond bracelet.

The boat slowed and Drew gracefully dropped back into the water.

"Who's ready for a beer?" Logan called.

A chorus of "me" had them heading back to the house, ending their skiing for the afternoon. Drew was going to grill fajitas for their dinner, but first they'd hang out on the deck and drink a beer or two, watching the activity on the lake as boats made their last few passes before dusk. It was a Saturday routine she'd grown to love.

She went inside to get a beer for everyone, then laughed as Logan stole up behind her. She sunk back against her for a moment, then turned in her arms, looping her own around Logan's neck.

"Good day?"

"Beautiful day," she said. "I love you."

Logan's eyes softened and she kissed her gently. "I love you too."

Peyton smiled as they pulled apart. "Have I thanked you lately for stalking me?"

Logan laughed. "Speaking of that, Emma invited us down to the coast next week. She's got a free room."

"Next week?"

"Yeah. You know, we haven't been down there."

"I know."

"We'll leave Monday."

"*This* Monday?" While she'd gotten used to Logan's spontaneity, she didn't think she could possibly juggle her schedule that quickly.

"I already called Susan."

"You did?"

Logan nodded. "She's taking care of your schedule. It's kinda like our anniversary, you know."

"I suppose it is."

Logan gave her that flirty, sexy smile that still made her pulse race. "So what do you say?" Another smile. "Come on. Sand. Surf. Shrimp." She wiggled her eyebrows. "And a sex toy. It'll be fun."

Peyton moved against her again, smiling as she kissed her. "Okay. But not necessarily in that order."

Logan laughed. "Of course not. Shrimp definitely has to come first."

Peyton's smile faded as Logan pulled her close, kissing her soundly. Her arms circled Logan's shoulders again and she sank into the kiss, moaning quietly as Logan cupped her hips and pulled her closer.

"Hey, what's a girl got to do to get a beer around here?"

They pulled apart guiltily as Drew came into the kitchen.

"Sorry," Peyton said. "My fault."

Drew laughed. "It's okay. We were smooching out on the deck too."

Peyton shoved Logan away. "Go on out. I'll bring the beer."

She smiled, watching them leave.

God, I love my life.

Bella Books, Inc.

Women. Books. Even Better Together.

P.O. Box 10543
Tallahassee, FL 32302

Phone: 800-729-4992
www.bellabooks.com